MW01252555

May 201?

Dear Alex

Thank you for
my dream a reality
no good deed remains
Love Freely, Live Freely and
be true to yourself.
much Gratitude & love
Bev Goodman

WOODFIELD,

a gated community

by Bev Goodman

WOODFIELD, a gated community is a work of fiction. Names, characters, places, and incidents either are the product of the author's imagination or are used fictitiously, and any resemblance to actual persons, living or dead, business establishments, events, or locales is entirely coincidental.

First Edition: April 2012

Copyright

Dedication

For their Infinite Loving Support

Melvyn, Alexandra, and Sydney

ACKNOWLEDGMENTS

Special thanks to Marcia, who shared so much of this journey with me, Hélène, whose friendship opened hearts, and Flora, whose feedback was invaluable, and who despite her enthusiasm insisted I continue with chapter two.

To my readers, thank you for your support. I wish you all boundless peace in your hearts.

And, last but not least, to the millions of women worldwide who feel as if they are living on the edge…waiting… waiting for the bottom to fall out!
This is to let you know there are many Lily White's around you, seek them out.

Thank You to Cover Artists
Photographer, Alix H. Luntz & Graphic Designer, Alexis Ely.

No one can separate what's together
But nothing lasts forever
End is what separates
Begins is what creates
And within fault lives "fate."

Sydney 2012

Chapter ONE

There is something to be said about the excitement of ordering on-line, and the anticipation of waiting to receive it. These were Ashley's thoughts as she approached the guard gate to her development. Her fingers drummed on the steering wheel as she counted down the days: Tuesday, Wednesday, Thursday... her thought trailed off, and came back again. Yes, it has to be today. I mean, after all I called them up, and told them if it wasn't here by Friday, just forget it. I need it for this Saturday, not for my vacation next month! They told her they would send it 'overnight,' but they did not have her size in stock, and had to have it shipped directly from the manufacturer.

"What do you mean?" she had asked, "Isn't this where the designer makes everything?"

"No Ma'am," the lady answered politely. "This is where we ship the products from."

Exasperated and confused, and really not interested in any of the how, what and why details, she demanded, "Well, you be sure it arrives by Saturday."

She drove smoothly through the 'residents only' gated line, as the machine registered her assigned sticker on the rear passenger window. She headed towards her sub-development within Woodfield, one of the trendiest neighborhoods in Woodfield Suburban Club, namely Cheshire. Most people who bought in Cheshire bought for the location. They would never live in the home. Heaven forbid live in a used home! No, they would either gut the house and redo the entire insides, or simply knock it down to the ground and rebuild the house of their dreams.

Ashley belonged to the former group. She and Joe simply fell in love with the bones of the house, when they saw it several years ago, but could not bring themselves to equally love the bathroom tiles in the master bath. If Ashley had to look at those ugly tiles on a Sunday morning after a hectic Saturday night out on the town she would never stop 'barfing,' she explained to her realtor.

Amanda, her realtor, who also lived in Woodfield, was quick to agree, then rolled her eyes as she turned away. Sometimes, Amanda thought, I wonder what these woman would do if tomorrow was the end of the world, what would she feel about those tiles then?

Ashley turned her white Mercedes into the driveway of number 1675. At the same time a car drove into her neighbor's driveway right next to her. It was Jennifer, the neighbor's nanny. Ashley had her eye on Jennifer as a babysitter since she moved to Cheshire. Cute, trendy Jennifer who always seemed to make the two little boys next door giggle and play peacefully all day. But Jennifer was well coveted by Ashley's neighbors, seldom giving Ashley the opportunity to even make conversation with her. Then she remembered her package.

Feeling a surge through her of uncontrolled happiness, Ashley blurted out aloud, "Oh, I'm so excited! Joe is going to love them! Absolutely love them, love them, love them, love them..." she trailed off.

She pressed the remote keyless entry button in her car, popped the trunk, grabbed her oversized purse, and turned off the car's engine. The garage doors opened obediently, and she hopped out her car. People who live in Woodfield usually leave their cars in the driveway during the day, and over time developed the habit of never using their front doors. And like everyone else in Cheshire, Ashley entered through the garage. I really have to call that guy Pam told me about. This garage needs to be organized.

"Nina, Nina, Nina." She yelled stepping into the kitchen. Nina was not in the kitchen. As Ashley walked through the house looking for Nina, her pitch heightened.

"Nina, Nina, Nina. Where are you?"

"I'm ba....a....ck," she sung happily, as if the whole world would be thrilled to see her return home.

Ashley found Nina attending to a very hysterical three year old Madison. Her younger son Joe, Jr., and eldest son David were not at home. Joe, Jr. was in kindergarten camp and David in summer day camp. David was twelve and in middle school.

"Oh. Hi, Miss. Ashley." Nina managed to get out, in-between Madison's flinging arms and angry disposition.

Madison's thick blond locks spilled over onto her face as she challenged Nina's actions, her spindly legs stomping as hard as they could on the bedroom floor, while her equally slender arms culminated in two small button fists.

"Were there any packages delivered today, Nina?"

"No, Miss. Ashley."

"Did you see the *FastEx* man drive through the neighborhood today, Nina?"

"Not that one stupid, the pink one, I want the pink princess one!!" demanded the child.

"No, Miss. Ashley."

Does she know anything other than the word 'no' wondered Ashley.

"What's wrong with you today Madison?" asked her mother.

With that Madison's, red and tear stained face turned to her mother standing at the door, she let out a string of words ending in 'the pink one' and 'I hate her.'

Nina was about to respond when Ashley stepped in exasperated, "Oh, for Heavens sake! Take her for a walk around the Woodfield circle! That will calm her down. Stop off at the park at the Clubhouse and let her run off some of this craziness. Oh, and Nina don't forget only healthy snacks. The

Club is giving out lemonade now, give her some of that if she gets thirsty."

Woodfield circle was a smoothly paved road and sidewalk, beautifully lined with colorful gardens and trees. Beyond it lay the original reason for Woodfield's location in the city, its state of the art golf course, the exclusive membership to which had a one year waiting list. The layout of Woodfield's gardens and golf course was so intricate it required a full time landscape company to take care of it, every day, six days a week. Workman not being permitted to enter the development on Sundays. The Woodfield circle also surrounded the infamous suburban clubhouse, recently reconstructed, and the reason for many of its new homeowners.

"Oh, and one more thing Nina. Before you go, please remove the supermarket packages from my trunk, and unpack them." With that Ashley disappeared from the bedroom doorway.

Behind Ashley's home was another home. Not directly behind it, of course, but figuratively speaking. Ashley had a very extensive swimming pool and patio entertainment area directly outside her home. This area was protected by a massive lanai overlay which cost them about $50,000 when they remodeled the home, but it was one of those *must have's* on Ashley's list.

"No-one can live here without one of those, not with all those nasty bugs that fly around in this place," Ashley told her husband at the time they bought the house. "Humid weather demands lanai overlays. It's essential for the children, Joe."

Anyway, directly behind the lanai was a thick hedge standing six feet tall, which hid the comings and goings of Ashley's family, and at the same time hid the comings and goings of the inhabitants behind them, which suited Ashley perfectly. The neighbor's house was also number 1675, but instead of 1675 NW 6th Street, it was 1675 NW 8th Street. Ashley had looked at that house during her house hunt, it was also on the market four years ago, but it never held any of the potential her house had, or so, she believed.

∞∞

The *FastEx* truck stopped at the Woodfield side gate. All delivery and service repair trucks were confined to the side gate. The side gate had simultaneously been re-modeled with the club house, to better accommodate the long line of service people who lined up faithfully, Monday through Saturday at 8 am, waiting to earn their keep for the day.

"Rob Eden," said the *FastEx* guy. "Here to deliver packages in Cheshire, Hamlet, and Lancaster."

"I.D." said the security officer.

What's with these security guys? Don't they ever train them? I'm a *FastEx* guy for Fucksake, thought Rob.

The very young security officer scanned Rob's driver's license, and in the same breath lifted the security bar allowing him entry into the development. Rob was tired. He had partied hard the night before with a bunch of his buddies. His best friend Bob had recently quit his job at *FastEx*, something about an English rowing expedition to Lake Malawi in Africa. Rob had chuckled to himself when he first heard about it, for him it sounded like a mission of self discovery. Bob had been hired by *FastEx* for a route in the same county as Rob, in a town directly north of this one. All cause for celebration. Only the celebration lasted till 4 a.m. regretted Rob miserably, but it's too late to cry over spilled milk. The sun shone brilliantly, its rays hitting him and the roof of the van in tandem, making his hangover seem heavier than normal. Only a dozen more packages and my day is done, Rob tried desperately to encourage himself.

∞∞

Brianna loved these summer days. She loved to feel the warmth around her. It allowed her to wear as little clothing as possible. After all, those new boobs of hers cost a fortune, she may as well show as much of them off as she could. Brianna had dropped her young sons off at daycare, and was about to get ready for her personal trainer when she noticed an oversized box outside her front door.

What's this, she thought? I never ordered anything. Well, not recently that I can recall. She picked up the package. 1675 NW 8th Street. Hah, funny she thought. She then read the name Mrs. Ashley Loveit. Who's that? She wondered. Not too deeply though, because the address was hers. No mistake about that. She looked around, bent down and picked up the box. *FastEx* delivery men were in the habit of leaving packages at the front door. This was Woodfield. No-one here had time to go to the *FastEx* office to actually pick up their packages if they missed the drop off.

Brianna was delighted with the contents, a beautiful pair of blue open-toe high heel platform sandals. She recognized the line, it was one of Gucci's latest styles. She then pulled out the sales slip: $1,995.00 PAID. I thought so, she smiled. She moved to a chair in her foyer carrying the box, sat down, removed the skimpy socks she was going to wear under her workout sneakers, and placed the right shoe on her right foot. She twirled her foot around to get a good look at the shoe from several different angles.

Nice, she thought, very nice. And, I absolutely love this blue color. She slipped the left shoe on. Gosh these fit perfectly. Brianna got up and walked the length of the foyer in the shoes. Comfortable, yes, she thought, very comfortable. I could go out this afternoon when the sitter comes and buy that cute little black and blue dress I loved the last time I was in *Model*, she thought. *Model*, was a high end neighborhood dress store for woman who had a little more than usual to spend. It did look awesome on me. I'll wear them on Saturday night, she thought, with her hands together across her chest as if in prayer, she squealed in delight.

Then, the doorbell rang its familiar ring. Oh, it's Johnny. Johnny was Brianna's personal trainer. She hurriedly pulled the shoes off from her feet, one at a time, and placed them haphazardly back into their box.

"Sorry, Johnny, won't be a moment," she said as she opened the door, "I just have to put on some shoes," she added pointing to her bare feet.

"Fine," Johnny gave his to-die-for smile, "I'll wait for you in the truck."

"*Okay*," responded Brianna with more than the usual excitement in her voice.

Johnny's truck housed his mobile gym, the side of which boasted how his personal devotion could lead you to be the 'best' version of yourself. Alongside his slogan were digitally enhanced life size photos of Johnny and two celebrity dancers, a tennis player, and a soccer player all exposing perfectly proportioned bodies toned in just the 'right' places.

∞∞

Brianna was in love with her new blue shoes, and as anticipated was able to purchase the little black and blue dress she was hoping for at *Model*.

Ashley, on the other hand, was devastated she never received her dream blue shoes. Her outfit on Saturday night would be so 'Eh' without those shoes. Joe tried to console her with promises to take her to New York to buy the shoes, but it didn't work. Ashley mourned those blue shoes, and no amount of money or service would be able to bring those shoes to her on time for Saturday night. There was only one thing she could do. Take herself down to the mall and buy a completely new outfit, only this time INCLUDING new shoes.

∞∞

Saturday rolled around quickly. Sitters were set in both households. Nina's sister, Olivia was stepping in for Nina, and

Brianna welcomed her teen neighbor, Lara, to watch her twin boys. Brianna stopped by the neighborhood nail spa, while Ashley ventured to a nail spa a little further away from home so she could meet a high school friend before her appointment for breakfast at a very trendy coffee bar on the seaside part of town. Joe was in the Woodfield Suburban Club gym, and Brianna's husband was locked away on the phone in his home office, after returning from a series of European meetings with prospective business investors.

Dinner that night was glorious for Brianna and her husband, Michael. They were joined by friends they had met through their children. The energy between the couples was relaxed and fun. Michael discussed his most recent investment product. Something, he had bought in the European market, and absolutely convinced to be a hit in the US market.

"Soon everyone will need one," said Michael.

Brianna glowed with pride hanging onto every word that left Michael's lips. The Lewis's were equally interested, although it was truly hard to tell with young people in this area of town. While they give you the impression they are deeply interested in what you were saying, almost in the same breath they would ask if you would like to take their most recent 'limited' edition motor vehicle acquisition for a spin.

Dinner ended around 11:00 and both couples agreed to move to the bar area of the restaurant. It would soon become busier, and the resident DJ would take over the music until the early morning hours. Drink orders were taken and phase II of the evening began.

At around midnight the Loveit's and their friends entered *Aqua*'s. The place was packed. Ashley chose *Aqua*'s because their smoking bar was located outside the restaurant, and well away from any open restaurant windows. She suffered from asthma, and there was nothing more of a drag than having to end an evening early because of an asthma attack. As they entered the bar area of *Aqua*'s, someone jumped up from a bunk seat at a table, and yelled her name.

"Ashley, Ash, Ashley over here." Ashley heard her name during that split second when the DJ was about to start a new song.

She turned to look and there she was, Amber Lewis, waiving her arms furiously in her direction, gesturing for her to come over. Ashley excused herself from her party and walked over to Amber. She knew Amber well, since she moved to Woodfield.

"Hey, Ash get some chairs and come join us."

Ashley explained that she was there with another couple, and if the other couple didn't mind then they would pull up some chairs. Soon all eight of them were huddled together around a rather small cocktail table, laughing and joking.

Ashley and Brianna got on particularly well. They discovered that they had similar interests, likes and dislikes. They both found raising kids a drag, and yet couldn't live without them. They had the same opinions about the right schools for their children, and they tended to like the same dress stores both locally and in New York. They had even gone to the same plastic surgeons. Ashley started to feel that she could really get close to this Brianna.

"So, where do you live Brianna?" Ashley asked her.

"Cheshire in Woodfield," answered Brianna. No, Ashley thought, a new friend right in my neighborhood.

"Meeee tooooo," shouted Ashley above the music.

And the two went off again on a tangent. How people can converse in a crowded rowdy bar was always a mystery. But somehow these two did. In fact, when Ashley and Amber visited the ladies room an hour later, Amber commented on how thrilled she was that Ashley and Brianna were getting along so well because she really took a chance in putting them all together. She also complimented Ashley on her outfit and matching shoes. Ashley mumbled between the toilet walls about how disappointed she had been because a pair of shoes she had ordered on line didn't make it on time for tonight, but Amber only got part of the story because she received a 'check in' phone call from the sitter.

When Ashley and Amber made their way back to the table they noticed that only Joe and Amber's husbands were sitting there.

"Where's everyone?" Ashley tried to shout above the music into Joe's ear.

"Out there," Joe yelled back, pointing in the direction of the dance floor.

~ 12 ~

Ashley turned to look towards the dance floor. She saw Brianna in the center waving her arms. Brianna sent Michael over to the table to call Ashley to the dance floor. Grabbing Joe's hand Ashley bounded over to the dance floor full of the joys of spring. She navigated her way through the crowd getting closer and closer to Brianna, until she was close enough …close enough to see her shoes – the blue shoes – the Gucci open-toe high heel platform sandals you couldn't buy locally.

Chapter TWO

The Woodfield women were saturated in the belief that their deepest desires were frivolous, and life was totally dedicated to the male species. This translated for them into having to look their best at all times, even if it meant going to the extreme, under the surgeon's knife or loading their bodies with all kinds of animal excretions, sometimes to the extent that their eyes would look as if they had crossed over into the goldfish species, not to mention their lips, and the skin on their face devoid of any natural elastic glow.

They had two important tasks, one, to keep up with every current fashion trend to enhance their husband's image when they entered a room, and two, to keep all males that were not intimidated by their good looks, drooling at the mouth, and at bay, which in turn also enhanced their husband's image. Surrounding these woman there were always a good amount of males shamelessly circling, awaiting the instant they could softly land where so many desired to tread, between their legs. And the male draw card was always the same: The potential to be their true love.

The men would profess an undying love for their prey, reeling them in with emotions in disguise, usually at the high risk of being caught by their wives or girlfriends. Once conquered, the females would then emotionally attach, for what they believed was forever, and the males would simultaneously emotionally detach, and be done, leaving another princess empty, shallow, and heartbroken. Usually after a few weeks of languishing, their husbands barely noticing as they themselves were too occupied targeting other females, they would go shopping, have a total makeover; hair, nails, clothes, perhaps a short trip or two to the plastic surgeon, all the time truly believing they had undergone a total transformation, and that their life from hereon out would focus only on their husband and children. Until, of course, the next potential prince.

These women were always searching. They had no idea what they were searching for, and every time they thought they had caught it, it would slip away, simply because they had no idea what it looked like or what they were looking for. It could bite them in the butt, and they would still call their best friends and ask - could this be the one? The small magical aspect which so escaped them all, was simply, LOVE.

None of them knew what it was, they had seldom seen it, or grown up with it. For them love came with prince charming, and their notions of prince charming were derived exclusively through the stories of Cinderella, and Snow White. Prince charming was out there looking only for them personally, and would be forever. All the tempting witches and dark forces were swiftly dismissed as mere distractions to the story.

The biggest failing, however, in the lifestyle of the Woodfield Women were the male species attracted to it, for they were even less whole than the women. So, it was a little like one empty vessel leading another empty vessel. The men, usually a part of this group, were from all areas of professional life; medicine, law, investment banking, sales. There was no one particular profile. They were often college educated,

WOODFIELD, a gated community

earning a very handsome salary, or had inherited one, or were master tricksters seducing others to believe they were living on an endless supply of funds. However, it wasn't until the women were forced to deal with the unbearable, they would finally become aware of this empty vessel they had actually chosen to date or in most cases marry.

The tempo in Ashley and Joe's car was anything but calm after leaving *Aqua*.

"I can't breath. I can't breath. I can't fucking breath," Ashley blurted out her chest heaving, and heaving.

"*Ash you need to calm down*. You really need to *calm down*. You going to have one of your asthma attacks. Please calm down. You just yanked me out of there. What the hell is with you?" Joe ended raising his voice at her.

"What the hell is with me! What the hell is with me? *How can you even ask me that?*" shrieked Ashley, her chest heaving even more.

"Ashley," Joe said a little less angry, and even more confused, "Why are you so intense?"

"Didn't you see those fucking shoes on her feet? *Huh*? *Huh*? The blue open-toe high heel platform Gucci sandals? *What are you blind*?" Ashley screeched.

"Are *you* kidding me?" Joe responded shocked. "You pulled me away from a perfectly fun evening for a pair of blue Gucci sandals? Have you *actually* lost your fucking mind?" Joe slammed his fist on the steering wheel.

~ 16 ~

"Joe, those aren't just any pair of blue Gucci sandals, those are the very same ones that *I* ordered online that didn't arrive! Those are the very same ones that *I* needed for my outfit *tonight*! Tonight, Joe! Don't you get it? She took my package! She stole them from me!" Ashley growled.

"That, Bitch! I knew it! It was too good to be true. All that sweet friendly chit chat, and all the time she was wearing *my* shoes! *My* shoes Joe! *My blue Gucci sandals Joe*!" Ashley rambled with all the vehemence in her.

"You have no proof those are your shoes Ashley. Last time I looked you two were chatting up a storm, and had a whole lot in common. You even whispered in my ear that you both liked the same things. So, she bought the same shoes as you Ashley. *So what*?" Joe rambled back.

"So *fucking what*? " Ashley's pitch once again took an upswing. "She *never bought* those shoes Joe, she *stole* those shoes Joe, she stole those fucking shoes from me!"

"You have no proof of that Ashley."Joe retorted.

"Yes, I have. You just have to look down at her feet!! They're on *her* feet!! Just look down at her feet Joe. That's all the proof you need! Just look down at that Bitches feet! How much proof does someone need to have Joe? To see the fucking receipt?" Ashley bellowed.

"Those are my shoes, and I want them back!" Ashley demanded looking right into Joe's face, and then turning away to face the passenger side window, and in a lower tone, "I have to work a way to get them back," Ashley's neurons had already begun connecting in an attempt to conspire some kind of revenge.

She was still heaving when she returned home. The minute Joe pulled the car into the garage, Ashley fled from it, slamming the door behind her. And again when she entered the kitchen, BAM went the door. Joe shuddered, simultaneously a set of motion detector lights turned on, directly outside the garage. In a desperate attempt to recoup his reality, Joe took his time to shut off the car's air conditioning, turn off the DVD player, and unplug his cell phone, before he turned off the car's engine, and entered the house. Over the years, he had learned it was much safer to keep a physical distance between himself and Ashley's ranting and ravings. He knew this was another one of those nights where he would have to check up on the children, and take care of paying the sitter.

Ashley stormed past the living room.

"Oh, hi Mrs. Loveit," said Olivia sweetly. Olivia turned down the TV as soon as she heard the banging of the kitchen door.

"Hi Olivia," Ashley responded tersely without breaking her stride or even looking in her direction.

"The kids were..," Olivia began, and before she could get the next word out Ashley, snapped, still not looking in her direction, "Joe has your money."

Ashley proceeded up the stairs, pounding her shoes heavily on the marble steps, her fury building with each step she took. Whether or not her children were sleeping was of no concern to her. She was even more angry than when she first got into the car to leave *Aqua*. Watch out Ms. Brianna. Watch out. Tomorrow I will put my plan into action. Just you wait, Ashley's thoughts threatened.

She pulled the new shoes from her feet keeping her balance by holding onto a newly upholstered bedroom chair. A chair, her decorator had insisted was looking rather shabby, and outdated. Ashley dumped the shoes where she stood, and with equal vigor proceeded to pull the clothes from her body, throwing some of them over the recently recovered chair, and the balance onto any piece of furniture within physical proximity to receive them, as she moved around the bedroom. She then headed for her en-suite, recently remodeled bathroom. Everyday since being completed, her bathroom had brought a satisfying little smile to the corner of her lips. But tonight, she failed to notice its tranquil glow enhanced by the floor to ceiling pane of glass, and the glaring full moon.

She cleaned the make-up off from her face, and applied a quick 3 minute mini-mask to her skin. While the mask was still drying, and Ashley rummaged through some drawers, Madison roamed into the bathroom rubbing her eye, *blankie* in hand. She took one look at her mother, and ran screaming out of the bathroom, and bounded for the bedroom door.

"Does that child ever stop ranting?" she questioned out loud to her reflection in the mirror.

Joe scooped Madison up into his arms as she was about to exit the bedroom, and he about to enter.

"Hey, come on little one, what are you doing up so late?"

"Hi Daddy," Madison squirmed delighted to be up in his big strong arms safe and away from the ghost she had just encountered in the bathroom. Joe took a giggling little Madison back to her bed.

Twenty minutes later Joe returned to the bedroom to find his wife lying prostrate on her side of their king size bed. She was mumbling furiously into her silk pillow – something about …"…You wait till tomorrow. You will be so sorry you ever set eyes on *MY* blue Gucci sandals Miss Brianna, or whatever the hell you call yourself."

Joe just shook his head, and proceeded into the bathroom.

Unfortunately, for Ashley, life had other plans for her the next day.

∞∞

A little earlier, and a few miles away Brianna and Michael's rhythm was very different. They left *Aqua*'s feeling acutely delighted with their evening.

"Now, that's what I call a fun evening," smiled Brianna, her arm linked with Michaels.

"Yeah, it was great wasn't it?" confirmed Michael.

"You look hot Babe," said Michael, "and I really like those blue shoes of yours. Where did you get them?" asked Michael.

"Thanks honey that's so sweet. The shoes were a surprise," answered Brianna, without explaining exactly what she meant by that, a surprise for her or for him? Michael never followed up. In fact, secretly he was totally disinterested in the history of the shoes, his testosterone was working up to a pitch, and right there, and then that was all he cared about.

"Let's go home to bed," he smiled while taking in Brianna's overall look.

"Are you making demands on my body, Michael?" Brianna teased, pushing her breasts out even further into the air.

"Aaahhh, my best financial investment yet!" Michael teased stroking her right breast in circular motions.

Brianna tittered, "You so funny when you drunk and horny, honey. Okay, let's go home."

On the way home, which was not a terribly long drive from *Aqua*, Brianna turned to Michael and said: "I really like Ashley. I hope I get to see her again soon. You know I think I will call Amber and get her number. Do you think that's too forward of me, Babe?"

"No," said Michael, "I liked her husband Joe a lot too. I think he and I could do some business together in the future." Brianna savored Michael's idea.

"Not, sure why she ran off that quickly though. She didn't even say goodbye," Brianna remembered.

"Oh, it was probably some emergency sitter issue. You know how that goes?" Michael said.

"Yeah, you're probably right," Brianna agreed, although something deep down within her didn't believe that to be the reason, but she couldn't think what else it could be at the moment, after all those drinks. She changed the subject.

"I really hope the boys had fun with Lara tonight. They always love her company. Aren't we lucky Michael? Two beautiful boys, great friends, a dream house, and we live in warm sunny Florida. Who would have thought? " Brianna trailed off. Michael had already tuned out at the words 'beautiful boys,' as he turned the car into Woodfield.

When they got home Brianna and Lara got into a very animated conversation about the boys. Lara reported they had been extremely well behaved, and deserved a treat the next day as a reward, and then the two of them chatted idly about insignificant issues in Lara's life, like what college she hoped to get accepted into, what major she was planning on taking, and if she had seen the cute summer orange and green sundress in the window of LU at Mizner Park. The atmosphere was light and happy in the home. Brianna paid Lara, and included a handsome tip (college fund she always told herself), and said goodnight.

She stopped by the boy's room, as she always did on her way to her bedroom. At first, she leaned against the door post marveling at the peace surrounding them, as they slept. Two little Angels, she thought. Their room was designed like an underwater submarine. She had been very particular about which designer she chose. She got a contact from *Benini*, a top of the line kids bedroom furniture store. They had a lot of Italian imports which she particularly liked. After she gave each one a kiss, softly blessing them with labels, "my sweet little doctor," and "my sweet little lawyer," she left the room.

Michael was already in bed when she reached the bedroom. No surprise there. He looks scrumptious, Brianna thought. "Oh, you are eager!" she teased as she passed by the bed.

"Mmmm…," Michael said, running his tongue across his upper lip.

She made her way into her dressing room… She and Michael each had one of their own… She slipped out of her cute black and blue dress, and then lifted it up to her lips to kiss and cuddle. "You made me look perfect tonight," she whispered to her dress. "And those shoes…," she continued, "a match made in heaven. My heavenly surprise! That's what I will call you from now on," she said addressing the shoes in the mirror, still on her feet, "my Heavenly Blues."

~ 23 ~

Brianna slipped into her blue Babydoll from La Perla, a Gaultier Createur. She loved it. This Canard Babydoll was a Jean Paul Gaultier's exclusive for La Perla– and best of all, for Brianna, it was inspired by Madonna's Blond Ambition Tour. How could she resist that? Madonna, to the Woodfield women was an icon. While they outwardly of course aspired to her sexy ways, they were all secretly mostly drawn to her glorious blaze of broad-mindedness, and expansive independence.

She inspected herself in the full length mirror. "Sexy as hell," she told herself.

As she bent down to take off her shoes, Michael called out from the bedroom. "Babe, don't take off those blue shoes. I want you to wear them to bed."

She could almost see that smile on his face. She went to the door of her dressing room and angled her leg around the post making it visible from the bed where Michael was lying.

"What, you mean these blue shoes, Babe?" she whispered tantalizingly.

"Wow!" he said, "I really *do* like those blue shoes. But not as much as I *love* those legs."

∞∞

The next morning, Joe gently tried pushing Ashley to wake her, "Ash, Ash, Ashley I have to tell you something. Ashley, you need to wake up."

Ashley groaned, covered her head with a pillow, moved away and then turned to face the other direction. "Go away." She grumbled.

"Ashley this can't wait."

"What?" Ashley blurted out annoyed, and half asleep. "What could be so important that you have to wake me?"

"Well, I couldn't tell you last night you were so angry over those damn blue shoes."

Oh, shit the blue shoes! Why the Fuck did he have to remind me again! That Bitch! Ashley thought again.

Interrupting her thoughts, "Ashley, listen, I can't come with you to Pam's today. I have to leave for New York."

Ashley lifted the pillow a few inches off her face, and turned to face Joe who was sitting on her side of the bed. "What? What are you saying? Pam is catering and asked me weeks ago. It's Independence Day Joe, the Fourth of July. No one works on the Fourth of July, Joe. The New York Stock Exchange is closed Joe. What the hell are you talking about?" She ranted.

"Well, I have an early morning meeting with a bunch of Hedgefund brokers on Wall Street, and I need to catch a plane for New York later today," Joe explained.

"The kids are going to be so disappointed. How can you do this to us Joe? And why didn't you tell me this before?

That way I could have told Pam there would be one less! What is your problem Joe?" Ashley whined, looking up at him.

"There's one more thing," Joe continued ignoring Ashley's questions, "I need you to run me to the West Palm Beach airport I couldn't get a service for today. I called too late. So, you may want to tell Pam that, too," Joe suddenly seemed distant.

"Ashley, I'm sorry," he said, and left the room.

Ashley arched her neck holding her head back on her pillow and let out a high pitched scream, "F U C K MY LIFE!!!"

Joe shook his head, and kept walking towards his den.

Later in the day Ashley dropped the kids off at Pam's. "I don't get men," she complained miserably to Pam. "He had all week to tell me this, and he lets me know this morning. What was he thinking Pam? I'm soooo sorry, I know you catered, and I feel bad."

"I know, I know, I know," Pam said nodding her head sympathetically, and then she ran amok with another one of her ex-husband ramblings, "It's like John, he would tell me he'd pick up the kids on Sunday, and then one hour before he is scheduled to pick them up, and I have already made *my* plans for the day he calls to say he can't make it, this or that has come up. And let me tell you Pam, this or that *was always* some *lame* garbage he needed to do! It's crazy, he doesn't get it, it's not me he's disappointing. I don't care if he dropped off the planet tomorrow, but the kids….*And*, when this used to happen before the divorce I would call that Court appointed Guardian Ad Litem woman, whatever her name was, and let her know exactly like the Judge told me to, how disinterested and obnoxious their father really was, and you know what she would say? 'He may have a perfectly good excuse Pam, let me call him. Let me call him!' Can you believe it? Call and speak to *him*! What exactly did she think? …." Ashley was tuning in and out as Pam rambled on.

There was something else, Ashley thought about Joe. I don't know what it is, she told herself, but there's something,…her mind wandered until...

"Mommy, can I go out and play with Justin in the pool, mommy, please, please, can I?" Madison nagged pulling at her mother's purse. Ashley had not put down her purse or keys upon arriving at Pam's because she was on her way out again to take Joe to the airport.

"Yes, but be sure the sitter has your floaty on though," Ashley instructed, but it was already to the back of Madison's small little body charging towards the French sliding doors leading to the pool. The word 'yes' was all Madison needed to hear. "Olivia," Ashley yelled, "be sure Madison has her floaty jacket on before she gets into the pool."

"Yes, Mrs. Loveit," Olivia responded, a little annoyed. If she didn't know that one by now!!! Olivia was the children's sitter on weekends, and most public holidays.

"Well, we will really miss you today, Ash. It's going to be so much fun. I asked that new couple. You know the ones rebuilding at 1112. The one with the double D's. You know which one?"

"Yeah," Ashley said, but she was already off down the front path moving towards her car. "Remind me to tell you about my blue shoes when I get back later," Ashley yelled back at Pam. Pam looked puzzled, then closed her front door.

Joe was ready to leave for the airport when she got back to the house. He threw his bag into the trunk and got into the passenger seat beside Ashley. Ashley backed out of the driveway, turned the car, and headed north towards the Woodfield gate. She stopped at the stop sign alongside the Oxford Park subdivision, and continued on her way. Neither of them said anything.

When Ashley turned onto the highway, the I-95 North bound, Joe began to talk looking straight ahead, "I'm sorry Ashley. I should have told you sooner. But look I need to tell you something."

Ashley ignored him. She didn't want to hear what he had to say. "When are you coming home Joe?" she asked irritated, and then continued onto another topic without even waiting for his response. "I feel so bad about letting Pam down like that. I feel like an awful person," Ashley stated.

"Ashley," Joe said firmly, "when Pam was going through that divorce of hers she let you down plenty. Don't you remember all those crying fits she used to have out of nowhere?

I think those went on for a year or more. It's not the biggest deal in the world." They passed the Lake Worth 10th Street exit.

Ashley remembered. Pam would call her at all hours of the day and night, hysterical most of the time over something John had said, or didn't say, or didn't do, or should have done. But, then Pam had been blind sided. Early one Monday evening, it must have been about 6 pm, Pam answered a ring at the door. To her surprise there was an officer standing on her doorstep. A few feet behind him stood a security guard from the Woodfield security. Pam was confused.

"Can I help *you*?" She had asked with her usual arrogant Pam self, *you're interfering in my life, and this better be good* attitude.

"Mrs.Pamela Cowin?"

"Yes," answered Pam curtly, no idea her life was about to change dramatically for the rest of her days.

"Consider yourself served, Mam," said the officer offloading a stack of papers about an inch thick into her hands.

"*What*?" a perfectly dramatic contralto pitch rang into the air, but the officer's follow up was simple.

"Have a nice evening Ma'am." He then turned, and left, with the Woodfield security guard in tow.

"*What*? What the hell do you think you're doing? This is some kind of mistake!" yelled Pam after the officer.

That was the first time Pam even knew her husband wanted a divorce. She slammed her door shut, and the fun began. Weeks and weeks, turned into months and months, as Pam endured court hearing after court hearing in an attempt to rape her husband of every penny she could. During this time, Ashley's phone never stopped ringing.

"Ashley, I have to tell you something," Joe said, bringing Ashley's attention back to the drive to the airport.

"What?" Ashley said, still annoyed by Joe's attack on Pam.

"I want a divorce. I've met someone."

Ashley felt like she had smashed her car into a solid brick wall. All the blood left her head, and she started to hyperventilate.

"I think I'm having an asthma attack! I can't breath! Get my medicine out my purse. Quickly I need it. Now!!" she yelled.

Joe pulled open her Artsy, personally monogrammed Louis Vuitton purse, and removed the inhaler from an inside pocket like a well-trained dog.

"Here," He said as he passed it to her.

Ashley inhaled twice, all the while keeping one hand on the steering wheel.

"Okay, so let me get this straight!" She was yelling and heaving all at the same time, "You have me drive you to the airport, under the pretense that you couldn't get a car service, to tell me YOU WANT A FUCKING DIVORCE!!! Have you actually lost your mind!! What kind of a cruel trick is this?"

Ashley continued in an accentuated squeaky mocking tone almost without taking a breath, "Oh, let the sweet, pretty little wife, mother of my children, come out for an Independence day spin to the *fucking* West Palm Beach airport so you can tell her YOU WANT A DIVORCE AND THAT YOU'VE MET SOMEONE ELSE? Am I meant to care? Am I meant to care that you have actually met someone else?"

Ashley furiously swerved the car off I-95 at the airport exit. The turn threw Joe forward in his seat, and activated his reflexes in his arms and hands.

With arms outstretched for leverage on the front dash he yelled, "Jesus, Ashley drive slowly you going to crash us. Calm the fuck down!"

"I'm sorry, what did you say Joe?" Ashley spoke mockingly in a low tone.

"Calm the *f...* down," She repeated quietly. "I'll show you calm the *fuck* down. I'll show you *calm alright*. No better still, I'll have *my lawyer* show you calm, Joe. Calm! Where do you actually get off Joe telling me to be *calm*? I'm the victim here or didn't you notice?"

Mockingly she continued, "I love you Babe. Please be my wife Baby. You're the sexiest girl alive, Babe, I can't live without you Baby. With this ring I thee wed Baby!!! With this ring I Thee Wed!" Ashley burst out sobbing.

They reached the airport terminal. Ashley was still crying. Joe was quiet. She stopped the car in a lane outside the Jet Gray airline terminal, and popped the trunk.

Joe sat quietly in his seat, turned to her and said, "I'm really sorry Ash. I didn't mean it to end this way. I will be home in a few days and we can talk some more."

"Oh, please take your time. There is *no* rush for you to come home," Ashley responded looking straight ahead both hands on the steering wheel ready to leave.

Joe stepped out of the car, went to the trunk and removed his bag, and set it down on the street next to him. He was about to proceed into the airport building when Ashley pressing the automatic button lowered the passenger side window, and called after Joe.

"Joe, this is the last free ride you're going to get out of me. After this it's going to cost you by the minute."

She pressed her foot down hard on the gas, and with a resounding screech sharply turned the car into the flow of traffic. She left Joe standing with his bag in the lane.

Chapter THREE

Woodfield women constantly walk around with an entitlement attitude, demanding to be first served or first attended to in any store, no matter how many people were waiting patiently in line before them. Although, acutely aware of this natural attitude they had nurtured over the years, they were convinced it demonstrated some form of assertive *female* power, girls always needed. And, invariably when someone in the line would express their discontent at their attempt to 'push ahead of others,' the Woodfield woman would stage a 'shocked look,' and explain briefly how they had no idea there was even a line in the first place. Fortunately, for them, this belief also protected them from the truth – other women only saw their behavior as ditzy, uncaring, rude and frivolous.

They also believed themselves to be hugely charitable and kind. When it came to PTA sponsored fundraisers they always did their part for society by sending in canned goods and non-perishables. They would give generously to those in need over the holidays by writing several checks, and they dedicated a large proportion of their time taxing their kids around town, dropping off their 'mini me's' at various imperative activities, designed to build their resume's for college, even if they were still in elementary school.

Ashley was no exception. She always considered herself a good, kind, and giving person. In her mind, she cared a great deal for humanity. She once told a nanny, who had donated many years of her life to the Peace Corps helping the very poor in countries like Zaire, Zimbabwe, and Niger, that although she cared for humanity she just didn't understand them too well, and why they just didn't get themselves a job if they had no money. The nanny never bothered to respond. After all, what do you say to someone who lives in an ivory tower separate from the world?

Moreover, and also conflicting with their understanding their behavior portrayed strong *female* power was another firm rule they held: They were life's victims in any event that ever arose. They were innocent bystanders at all times pulled, pushed and thrown about by the tides life dished out to them. They considered their biggest offense to be when they cursed at some 'idiot' driver who was trying to steal their parking space outside the supermarket. After all, they would only park in a spot down the center lane that lead directly into the supermarket's front door, everybody knew that.

∞∞

Today, Ashley's life had developed another crevice, one which had delivered a hard blow to her. She was a true victim! Blue shoes, her first crevice, had been promoted to her brain's neuron waiting room, while she tried to focus on more immediate matters. With a crevice, comes a time to reminisce. Too much reminiscing, and a new fissure may form. It is much like the plates in the Earth, one moves, and causes another to dislodge.

Ashley wasn't thinking about the blue shoes after leaving Joe at the airport. She drove around mindlessly before she eventually took the highway home.

"I want a divorce, I've met someone, I want a divorce, I've met someone, I want a divorce, I've met someone..." She kept repeating in a sing-song tone. She then started to pound on the steering with her left hand. Where does he get off doing this to me, to us! This happens to people like Pam, not me! How did this actually happen? He did this behind my back! How is this even possible? What's happening to my Fucking life? First someone steals my blue shoes, then Joe wants a divorce!

Suddenly, Ashley's thoughts reverted back to high school. She had known Joe in high school. He was her first love. She had lost her virginity to him. He was the jock, and she the cliché cute little cheerleader. Everybody envied them. The hottest boy on the team was hers. But then she remembered some of the rumors she had heard. She refused to listen to them at the time, but now all these years later, perhaps they had some truth to them. How stupid had she been, if she had only listened then, maybe she wouldn't be in this mess today. Too late she thought. But it didn't stop the flood of high school memories.

One memory in particular kept playing out in her mind. They were seniors. It was a Friday. She had made plans with Joe to meet him in the locker room at 5:30 after his practice game. The game actually finished at four but Joe said he needed time to clean up. She never thought that his request of an hour and a half was particularly long. Especially when you measure it against her two and a half hours to get showered, changed and apply her makeup.

They were planning to go to his house that evening, and have sex, because his parents were out of town, and his brother was having a few friends over. Ashley killed time hanging around Moorestown's Shopping Village until 5:20 pm. The Village was located directly across the street from Moorestown High.

She had been a little early, but didn't think it would matter. Maybe she and Joe could make out in the locker room. The thought excited her and she quickened her pace. But then as she approached the locker room she saw Pam leaving. Pam, her best friend. In hindsight, Pam looked a little disheveled. Her hair which was usually pin stripe straight, was kind of messy, uncombed, and tousled. Her shirt was tucked half in and half out her jeans. Another big *no, no* for *preppy* Pam. She also had no lip gloss on, Ashley suddenly remembered. Pam would never be seen without lip gloss on her lips. She was obsessed the boys always found her ravishing and never failed to continually remind Ashley.

Pam seemed shocked when she saw Ashley walking towards her. "Pam?" Ashley said in a questioning tone as she got a little closer, "what are you doing here? And, why do you look like that?"

"Oh, Hi, Ash. I was just, I was just, uuhhh, looking for my binder," Pam said.

"In the boy's locker room?" Ashley had asked surprised.

"Uuhh, yes. I just spoke to Rob. I gave him my binder to copy stuff." She was twirling her hair with her right hand. "And he said he thought he may have left it in the locker room, and that I should go down to school and look for it." Pam finished, again accelerating the speed of her last few words.

"Well?" Ashley had said.

"Well, what?" Pam said shrugging her shoulders.

"Did you find it?" Ashley said irritated.

"The binder, you mean?" Pam said.

"Yes, Pam. The binder! Didn't you say you lent Rob your binder?" Ashley said exasperated.

"Ahhh, no I didn't find the binder," and she raised her hands up to exaggerate she didn't have anything in her hands.

"Well, you'd better go home, and call him," Ashley said. "Oh, by the way, did you see Joe in there?" Ashley asked as Pam was about to rush off.

"J-o-e?" Pam repeated slowly.

"Yes, Pam, *my* boyfriend, Joe?" Ashley repeated again irritated.

"No. Bye Ash," and Pam ran off.

When Ashley entered the locker room Joe was at his locker with a white towel about his waist and dripping with water. "Hey, Babe he said. You look hot. Come here."

Something seemed wrong. She remembered feeling it in her gut. Why was Joe still wet from showering, the practice game ended at four. He had plenty time to shower and be dried by this time. It must have been at least 5:35 p.m. by then. Ashley cursed aloud in her car. How stupid had she been? She remembered Joe's response when she asked him if he had seen Pam leave the locker room.

"This locker room?" he had said innocently, as if surprised Pam would have ever been in the boy's locker room. Ashley realized now, how many years later, what a mocking tone he was actually using with her?

"No, Babe. Why would *she* be in here?" he answered non-chalantly, tacking on a question in an attempt to make her second guess herself.

"She said she was looking for her binder she had loaned Rob," Ashley answered. Joe shrugged, brushing it off, and proceeded to dress.

They followed through with their plans that night, and went back to his house. They had sex on the floor of his parent's bathroom, after smoking some of their marijuana joints they had found in the cabinets under the sink. Usually Joe would not have smoked pot, he was a hard core athlete, but he said at the time he didn't have to worry because he had already been accepted into a college up north, on a full scholarship because of his athletic abilities. Another strange thing, Ashley remembered.

And, as she continued to recall more and more of her past the worse it seemed to get. The next Monday, Ashley had class with Rob.

"Rob," she called out, "I want to ask you something."

Rob ambled over to her desk smiling and salivating, "Ask me anything, Ash," he said his eyes fixed on her soft rounded breasts cupped in her pale pink sweater. Rob always had his eye on Ashley. Thinking back now, she should have slept with him.

"Did you borrow a binder from Pam?" Ashley had asked matter of factly.

"Er, no, why?" he scratched his head as if he had to think about it.

"You sure?" She pressed.

"Yeah, cause I'm sure Ash, why would I lie about that?" He shrugged. "Why are you even asking me anyway?"

"Oh, nothing," Ashley said. As Rob was about to move in closer, she turned on her heels and walked away.

But Ashley was furious at the time. She remembered going to the lockers, grabbing Joe by the arm and pulling him aside. "Are you cheating on me?" she had asked him, a little louder than normal causing the usual bitchy girls to giggle as they passed by.

"Now, Ash, why would I do that?" Turning to face her, and simultaneously pulling her towards him and cuddling her, he added, "You're all the girl I need, so why would I look anywhere else?" Right then, and there she lost all her investigative powers, and surrendered to her puppy love, as easily as she had lost her virginity to him.

How stupid, she repeated reprimanding herself, as she sped south along the highway. While I was killing time at Moorestown's Shopping Village Joe was fucking Pam. How stupid, stupid, stupid could I have been?

She remembered something else too. A pretty blond girl once tried to tell her to keep an eye out because her boyfriend was a little too friendly to her during class, and had been endlessly calling her house trying to reach her on a weekend Joe was supposed to be out of town playing ball. Seems like he was playing a different ball game to what Ashley had thought.

"You need to keep an eye out," she told Ashley. "Everyone is talking about it."

"What a bitch," Ashley had branded her to Pam. Yes, Pam of all people! She now recalled. She had ranted to Pam that this girl was after her boyfriend, and this girl thought by telling her he was after her, Ashley would think Joe was to blame.

Ashley's heart sank. All those girls who giggled when they overheard her that day mouthing off at Joe, they knew. They all knew what a cheat he was. Only she didn't. Ashley headed towards Atlantic Avenue. She forgot she was meant to go back to Pam, and pick up the children. She remembered there were a lot of bars along Atlantic Avenue, and she needed a drink, yes, she needed a drink badly, she told herself.

She drove slowly along Atlantic Avenue. Now where about is that bar? Aah, there it is, she told herself. She turned down a side street to look for a parking. Minutes later she was sitting on a bar stool in the *Apple Martini*. She ordered a Bluetini. Gulped it down and then ordered another. By her third she was beginning to feel better. She liked the bartender. He was cute she thought, and then she remembered she was *free* to think so.

"Hey," she said to him, "how many wives do you get sitting at this bar in a week drinking because their husbands have asked them for a divorce?"

He turned to look at her, and smiled. "Why, is that what happened to you today?" he asked.

"Yes. What's the time now?" she asked. Ashley had lost all track of time.

"Seven to be exact," he said.

Ashley couldn't believe it. Where had she been? She returned to her conversation with the bartender. "Well, I don't know exactly what time it was when he asked me, an hour or so ago. This is all he said. I'm sorry Ash. I want a divorce. I've met someone. Nice Independence Day gift isn't it!" Ashley screeched waiving her glass in the air.

Then she started to laugh. "He probably thinks he'll get his independence on Independence Day! He probably thinks it's a fucking Independence Day holiday for him!" She seemed to be the only one who caught her joke.

"Yeah, that's a downer. Stupid guy. Why would he want to do that to you?" the bartender said, obviously trying to make Ashley feel better about herself, and yes, he had been witness to this trauma many times during his hours bartending.

"No, no, no, not stupid guy," Ashley took a sip of her drink, "stupid girl for wanting to marry him in the first place." Ashley said with resolve. "He's not the first to cheat on me you know," she continued. "My last husband, my eldest son's father was also a cheat. He was just more open about it. I had to eventually leave that one. Can I have another one please?" She pushed her glass toward the bartender.

"I'm sorry but this has to be the last one I serve you. You're cut off! Otherwise, I could lose my job," he said to her.

With her pointer finger wagging from side to side she said, "No, no, no, we wouldn't want that now would we. Okay last one," Ashley promised with a drunken smile.

She reached for her Blackberry in her purse, and looked for Olivia's name in her contacts, highlighted the name and dialed her number. "Lucky for these phones," she said to the bartender, waiting for Olivia to answer, "otherwise how would we remember the number to call after a few drinks?" She giggled, "Oh, hi Olivia?"

Olivia overheard the tail end of her giggling,"Yes, Mrs. Loveit," she answered. She thought it strange she could hear loud music in the background, because she knew Ashley had gone to the airport.

Ashley squirmed at hearing her last name. Loveit, how proud she had once been to own it. Ashley could hear a lot of laughter in the background. She could make out Pam's usual high pitched laughter. "Bitch," she said out aloud.

"I'm sorry Mrs. Loveit?" Olivia said rather surprised.

"No not you Olivia," Ashley corrected quickly, "someone here. I'm held up Olivia. I need you to take the children home. Tell Pam I'm held up, and I cannot get back to even pick up the kids. Be sure the younger ones have a bath, give them dinner and put them to bed. Tell David he needs to take a shower before bed. I'm going to be late. I have something to do. I have a lot to do. I'm very busy right now."

"Is everything *Okay* Mrs. Loveit?" Olivia asked.

"Now, Olivia if everything wasn't fine do you think I would tell you?" Ashley responded rudely.

"Okay Mrs Loveit. I will do as you say."

Olivia never bothered to respond to Ashley's rudeness. Baby sitters like Olivia were very used to seeing and hearing their female employers drunk on many an occasion after returning from a night out. What was unusual this time though, was that Olivia's employer sounded distressed, confused, and quite upset. Olivia had a feeling something wasn't right, but she brushed it off. She didn't mind having to stay on later, more hours meant more money.

Ashley left the bar after her third drink, as promised, and returned to her car. To her delight she was able to get in, and drive quite confidently. Must be those Blue Martini's she thought to herself. She was referring to her heightened confidence. Smiling triumphantly she maneuvered out of the parking, and drove herself the quarter mile to the ocean. The ocean was at the end of Atlantic Avenue.

She found a parking along the beach road, got out her car, and walked without purpose along the beach. She stopped, took off her shoes, and continued to walk. Her mind was blank. She felt better. She passed couples holding hands, people walking their dogs, and small children running seemingly pointlessly up and down the beach, laughing and joking. Then there were the obsessed exercise freaks who ran up and down the beach sweating, passing her one way then passing her again a half hour later running in the opposite direction. Who runs at night? Ashley thought. You have to have absolutely nothing to do with your life if that's what you do at night.

She had no idea how long she had been walking, before she decided to head back to her car. Then she remembered his words, "I want a divorce. I've met someone." She suddenly felt like having another drink. I'll stop off at the bar right opposite where I parked my car, she thought. And so she did, ordered a

Rum and Coke, and drank it down quickly. The walk had made her hot. She could feel the sweat skulking down her back. She was sure she was coming down with something. I'm going home she thought. All I want is to curl up under my comforter and die.

After another rum mix, Ashley returned to her car, and drove in the direction of Woodfield Suburban Club. Heading west and right before entering Woodfield it happened.

"Oh, fuck, Oh, fuck, Oh fuck!" Ashley yelled out loud. In her rear view mirror flashed the red and blue lights, almost blinding her.

"Please, pull over to the curb. Pull over to the curb," the officer bellowed through his P.A. system.

"What the fuck was that?" Ashley circled her head around disoriented. The next thing the flashing lights were right alongside her. She looked briefly to the left. It was a police car. She could just barely make out the officer inside who was making sweeping movements with his arm, gesturing for her to pull over.

Then she heard it again. "Please pull over, please pull over to the curb lady." She slowed down, and headed towards the road's shoulder. She stopped parallel to the oversized neon sign advertising River High School.

Oh, my f... I've been drinking. He's going to know. What am I going to do now? What did that lawyer friend of Joe's say about being picked up by the cops for a DUI? She tried to race through the neurons in her brain to find the connectors to the conversation she recalled at dinner a few months back. All she could recall, was don't open your window, don't admit to anything, and refuse the breath test. Oh, I hate you Joe. You pig! This is all your fault!

"Ma'am, can I see your license? Ma'am? Ma'am, can I see your license?" Ashley turned her face in the direction of the voice. She looked to the left and then up. She could easily hear him through the closed window.

Oh, yes she knew this officer, Officer Red Ends. He had worked that neighborhood ever since she moved there. Some said he had been working that corner for twenty years. He would set speed traps and catch all those *don't give a shit about your kids* people every week, when the school caution lights were flashing, telling drivers school children were out on the streets. At least that is what Ashley and her friends called them. There were two schools directly outside Woodfield, a middle and a high school. Both rated the best schools in the county. Ashley and her friends made a point to always fervently wave hello to Officer Ends when they passed him by, and they made an extra effort to greet him when he had caught one of those *people* with his laser speed contraption thingy. Maybe he will remember me, and let me go, because I'm one of those caring Woodfield residents, she thought.

Ashley acknowledged Officer Ends, and said, "One minute officer I have to look for it." All the while keeping her window up.

She opened her wallet, and fumbled through her cards. The officer waited patiently at her window. Where the hell is that stupid driver's license? It's the card with the picture, she kept telling herself. Look for the picture. Her head was beginning to pound, not as loudly as her heart at that moment, but enough to make her touch her forehead.

The card with the picture, picture, picture…There it is. She opened her driver side door and slipped the card to the officer. Then she quickly shut the door.

"Ma'am," he said seconds later, "Ma'am. This is a credit card. This is not your driver's license."

Oh, shit! What the hell! She turned to look at the card he was holding at eye level for her to see.

"I need your driver's license. Ma'am…" he looked at the name on the credit card, "Ms. Loveit."

"Yes, officer. I'm sorry. They all look the same in my wallet." Ashley returned to fumbling through the cards.

"Finally, you little shit!" she mumbled under her breath pulling her driver's license from her wallet in one grand swoop. She opened the door again, just slightly, enough to pass her license to the officer. He took it and simultaneously gave her back her credit card.

"I'll be right back," he said, and disappeared.

Ashley slumped over her steering wheel and continued to mutter to herself. "Just take me now G-d. You don't need me down here. I'm no use to anyone here. Life sucks. Take me. What the hell. Here I am G-d giving you a freebee to take someone. No plans. You didn't even have to plan any tornadoes, or hurricanes. It's an easy one G-d. What the hell is with you today?" She looked up at the roof of her car.

"Why did you introduce me to idiot Joe again, and so soon after the other idiot in my life, Joseph? Shit why doesn't this officer just let me go! I'm good. He needs to be catching those *don't give a shit people*, not me."

Ashley wasn't sure what happened right after that. She seemed to have passed out or stepped out of time. Then she heard voices shouting but they seemed far away from her. She turned to her left in what seemed like the direction in which the voices were coming from. Two gun holsters. Funny how can one officer have two gun holsters, she wondered. Oh, she giggled, there must be two officers now!!! Of, course!

The officers tapped lightly on her car window. "Ms. Loveit. Ms. Loveit. Are you ok? Ms. Loveit."

Ashley turned to look at the officers. "Yes," she responded absently.

"Ma'am we need you to step out of your vehicle."

"No can do," she said softly to herself.

"Ma'am, we would like you to take the Field Sobriety Test. Ma'am we need you to step out of your vehicle now!" They persisted.

Oh, I've seen those tests on the movies, thought Ashley. You have idiots walking a line and pointing to their noses. No way in hell I can do that test in these beautiful new Louis Vuitton Marbella's. She remembered how insistent she was on ordering the vert color she had seen online. When she later called the company to check on her order the woman kept trying to sell her the black patent leather ones. Now why would I want a black shoe when I live in sunny Florida Miss, Huh? And it's summer, I need green and white. I don't wear black toe polish in summer. I wear green or French. So, let's forget the black, okay? Gucci had given her a refund for the blue shoes she never received. So, what better way to get back at them than to go to their competition?

"Ms. Loveit, please step out your car," the officers continued.

Oh, my Fuck I'm still here. Okay G-d. You can't deal with this? What the job not big enough for you or something? Her mind ranted mockingly. What this all a little tooooooo much for you? Fine. I will just have to show you how it's done.

Talking through her car window Ashley said, "Now officers, I'm not going to step out my car, and I'm not going to do your little walking tests, or nose tests, or any of your little tests, so why don't you just let me go home. I live right there," she pointed ahead, "look across the street see, the Woodfield Suburban Club sign. *That's* where I live! You can follow me home if you don't believe me."

"Ma'am, if you refuse any of the tests I have to take you down to the station."

Oh, for f..sake. Okay. Okay. Okay. G-d feel free to jump in here!! Any Time!!! Where the hell are you? Oh, yes that's typical another man letting me down. Great.

"Ma'am, we cannot let you drive. Please just step out of the vehicle and come with us."

"But I've driven all this way anyway, and I just have an eensy weensy way to go, and I'll be home boys. See?" She pointed again reassuringly at the Woodfield sign. "Anyway, I can't just leave my car here on the side of the road," Ashley protested in frustration.

"Don't worry Ma'am we'll take care of it. You'll get the car back. Just step out of the vehicle and come with us."

Sounds like Joe, Ashley thought. Just step into my life and follow me. I'll take care of you princess. I'll take care of everything. Just come along. Follow the yellow brick road with me. And with these thoughts Ashley began to sob uncontrollably. Head in hands, slumped over the wheel, she let it all out. "I can't," she said between sobs. "I just can't take it. It's all fake!"

"Ma'am. Please step out of the car," the officer pleaded yet again.

Ashley didn't hear the third police car with its flashing lights pull up alongside her. Minutes later a female officer stood at Ashley's window.

"Miss. My name is Officer Rose. I'm here to help you. Look I know you're upset. It's Okay. Everything's going to be okay."

Ashley's curiosity got the better of her, and her left eye peered out from between her fingers. She wanted to catch a glimpse of this officer with a female voice.

"Please Miss let me help you," Officer Rose continued to beseech.

Ashley sat back up in her seat. Her eyes were circled in large black mascara rings and her cheeks streaked with foundation. She looked like what could be a Jackson Pollock canvas at its origin. She breathed in deeply. What choice did she have? She couldn't sit cooped up in her car forever. No matter what that stupid lawyer had said. After all, it figures he's another man.

"Are you going to arrest me, Officer, if I come out of my car?" Ashley asked her tone beginning to show signs of relent.

"Look Miss, I'm not going to lie to you. You are in no condition to be driving a car. We will need to take you down to the station."

"Okay," said Ashley, "but no tests. Got it? No tests."

"Got it. No tests." Officer Rose echoed, at the same time sending affirmative eye signals to the male officers informing them she was successfully breaking down the driver's resistance.

The moment Ashley stepped out of the car she went into autopilot. She followed all instructions that were given to her flawlessly, except of course when they tried to get her to take the breathalyzer tests later at the station.

"When do you read me my rights?" she asked as she sat in the rear seat of the police vehicle, arms cuffed behind her back. No one responded. The officers ignored her and talked amongst themselves. She then looked around, taking in her total experience sitting in the back of a cop car. Even when she grew up in a big city she never had this privilege. And now here she was, Ashley Loveit, Resident of Woodfield, in the back of a police car! I so hope Joe drives by and sees this! Oh, but of course he can't, he's probably too busy drinking coffee at Marocchino's on Fifth with that new girlfriend of his. Waaaay toooo busy to be concerned about meeeee. Ashley edged forward in her seat.

"Hey," she motioned with her chin towards Officer End behind the wheel, "you married?"

"Yes, Ma'am. For ten years now," he responded.

"Any kids?"

"Yes Ma'am, two, as a matter of fact – boy and a girl."

"You ever cheat on your wife officer?"

"No, Ma'am."

Liar, Ashley thought.

"Well, don't," she said, "unless you want her to end up like me, in the back of a police car." The officers looked at one another, and Officer Rose raised her eyebrows. They had heard it all. A few years on this beat and there are no more surprises. This place was full of 'them loony-tunes.'

The local jail was not the experience Ashley was hoping for. They removed all her jewelry, had her sign for it, and had her sit in a barren *puke colored* holding cell, as she later described it to her lawyer. And not the lawyer she had met with Joe, either. He was tainted, he was Joe's friend. No, another one – a female. Perhaps she would have some kind of understanding about the workings of this crappy world, Ashley thought, as she sifted through the criminal lawyer ads she received a few days later in her mail box.

Seven a.m. the morning after Ashley was arrested, she was officially charged. She was brought before a rather dull *enough-of-this-job-already* judge. Two criminal counts: Reckless driving and DUI. First, she insisted upon telling the Judge she was not guilty and there had been some terrible mistake, and then she turned her attention to the aesthetics of the jail sharing her thoughts about the jail cell, and informing the Judge the cell needed a new paint job, and she knew just the designer for the job. The Judge wasn't even remotely interested. He only raised his hand motioning her to stop talking, like her friend's little girl does when she doesn't want to hear what you have to say, "talk to the hand 'cause the ears aren't listening."

"Next case," was all he said, dismissing Ashley.

What's with these people Ashley thought, it's like a conspiracy club? No-one listens to you.

Even the public defender wouldn't listen to her. Reading the form she had been asked to complete he said, "We can't provide you a public defender, Miss. Your husband makes too much money."

When she opened her mouth to speak, to tell him that he was soon to be an ex-husband, he called out someone else's name. She was left literally with her mouth hanging open.

The woman next to her shrugged and said, "That's the way it is around here, may as well be dead."

"That's ridiculous," Ashley blurted out.

The woman next to her merely shrugged again, "I wouldn't waste my breath lady, just get yourself a lawyer. Them kind only speak to them own kind."

"I got to get out of here. I have kids," was Ashley's response.

"I hear ya," resonated the woman next to her.

An hour and a half later Ashley was called to a clerk's desk, given back her personal belongings, and told she could leave.

"Did you park my car out front?" she asked the clerk that released her.

"What?" laughed the clerk. "Ma'am, there's no valet here! There's the number you can call to get your car back." She pointed with the back of her pen, the one she had been chewing on, to a half sheet of white paper that had a 561 number printed in bold type. There was a messy pile of them lying around on the top of the counter. Ashley stared down at the number.

"Great," Ashley said out aloud, "So this is taking care of my car?"

"And what's this?" she held up the yellow court paper, waiving it furiously as if about to reprimand her child for a bad grade.

"What am I supposed to do with this?" she asked irritated, her left hand on her left hip.

"Give it to your lawyer," answered the clerk in a mellodramatic tone, mimicking Ashley's hand on the hip.

"And, how am I supposed to get to my lawyer if I can't even get home?" Ashley stated thinking she had finally stumped this clerk. She was still standing with her hand on her hip, and her jewelry returned to its rightful place – on her body.

The clerk shrugged her shoulders, "Why don't you just try calling someone from your cell phone?"

Ashley reached into her purse to pull out her cell phone. *Thank you Blackberry.* She gave her phone a kiss. *What would I do without your standby mode. No doubt my old phone would have been long dead to the world by now.*

After making that mind blowing 'thank heavens for that special Blackberry Torch feature' observation, Ashley continued to stand at the clerk's desk staring at her phone. Who would she call? She can't have any one of her friends pick her up, she was a mess. And, from this place! Heaven forbid! What was she going to do?

"Ma'am, can you step aside, I need this space. I have to check out some other hotel guests," she scoffed at Ashley's reality.

"What?----yes---," Ashley said absentmindedly. She scooped up all her things, and stood looking for a way out of this hell hole, when the clerk behind the desk lifted her arm and pointed the way to the exit door without saying another word. Submissively, Ashley moved towards it.

The clerk only shook her head. "What world do these people live in?" She asked herself aloud.

Ashley went to her contacts and called the one number she called several times a day, every day. "Mom. It's me. Mom I need you now," Ashley said, tears streamed down her face as she stepped out into the sunlight. Simultaneously, there was what initially seemed like an applause. It was coming from the building next door. Higher up, about the Sixth or Seventh floor. As she gave the noise her attention she could then hear it wasn't really an applause but a series of 'cat' whistles from what sounded like a dozen men or so.

"Hey, baby."

"Why don't you come up here and visit us now that you free."

"Woah, babe."

"What is that?" her mother asked on the phone, "I can't even hear you. Ash? Ash?"

"Hold on a moment, Mom. I will be right with you."

At that moment an officer walked by. "You may want to move yourself to this side lady," he pointed to a shady area to his left, "out of sight of those inmates up there. That is, if you want to hear anything on that phone of yours."

Joe should have only heard that, Ashley thought. All those men after her! Yes sir, she's still got something, even in this condition! Ashley turned to the building where the inmates were, lifted her head up, and shading her eyes with her one hand, smiled a huge smile, and waved the broadest wave. She didn't remember her makeup was still smudged from the night before.

"Bye guys," she said. With that came another avalanche of cheers and whistles. This made Ashley feel content. She was now ready to move over to the shade and speak to her mother.

"Mom?" She began to give her mother snippets of the previous night's events. A few minutes later Ashley's mother and father had determined that they would fly down to Florida in the next day or so, help her with the kids and the hiring of a lawyer, or two. By the sound of it Ashley needed more than one, thought her mother.

Her mother began to blather, "Darling, you've been through so much. Just call a cab and go home. Have a nice shower and take a rest. I'll call the sitter, and let her know that you were held up and decided to stay over at a hotel last night rather than drive home from the bar. I'll tell her to take the kids to the club and give them breakfast, and then take the two smaller ones to the park. Joe, Jr. won't be able to make school." Ashley lost focus for a few seconds, and then tuned back to her mother's voice.

"...If she can't stay later I will have her drop the kids off at the Woodfield kids care center, and you can go and pick them up from the club later. I'll have her leave you a note. We'll speak later. Go home Ash, and don't you dare call that big-mouth friend of yours Pam, unless you want your story on the notice board at the Woodfield clubhouse!"

Uggh, Pam, Ashley thought.

Ashley used her Blackberry to find a local cab company, and orchestrate herself a ride. She found a bench in the shaded area, sat down, and for what felt like the first time that morning breathed in the fresh air. Then a woman stepped out of the same door Ashley had twenty minutes earlier. Again, she heard the avalanche of cat calls and whistles. Are you kidding me, are you all blind? She thought. Have you seen what this woman is wearing? What she looks like? That has to be the ugliest dress, and it's probably an off the rack S-mart special, and you cheer her on as much as you cheered me on!! What is happening here? G-d what kind of world is this?

With that internal dialogue came a soft, vaguely familiar saddening of her heart. *I'm special. Why can't anybody see that?*

The white limo pulled up alongside the curb. Ashley quickly slipped into the back seat. The same sixth or seventh floor tune replayed from the building next door, but this time it didn't pick up a response from Ashley.

"Don't worry Miss. I will have you home in no time. You just relax," he said. And then he said, "First time in jail Miss?" But, Ashley didn't hear, she was already asleep.

Chapter FOUR

The Woodfield women had an uncanny way of being able to keep things very private. They would go to the extreme to keep their personal life as secret as possible and away from the prying eyes, and ears of even their nearest and dearest friends, *especially* their nearest and dearest friends. That is probably because they are all a part of the inner gossip circle, and only too well aware of how truly destructive it can be.

Taylor Aims had first discovered her husband's infidelity through the inner gossip circle. Pam had casually said she had seen Taylor's husband Paul, at a business lunch with a sweet young brunet that day, and commented on what a good job her plastic surgeon had done on his lips. Paul was meant to have been out of town for the past few days. The result was not a pretty picture. Everyone had to work hard at calming Taylor down that night with their wise words, which were highly affective as a result of personal experience living daily lives with lying and cheating husbands. Secretly, therefore, no one was particularly shocked that Taylor's husband was being unfaithful to her. At the same time, no one let on they were living with the same plight Taylor Aims had just begun to experience.

But the strange thing about these Woodfield women was that they had an inner strength which seemed to emerge during times of trouble, and while flippantly played out in the real world, actually accomplished positive results. Not always the results they wanted which allowed them to move in and out of their victimhood mode as they needed, but results that seemed to land them back on their feet somehow.

∞∞

Joe returned mid-afternoon Friday. He found Ashley in front of the mirror in their bathroom applying her mascara.

"What are they doing here?" He questioned in a frustrated high pitch tone, with an outstretched arm towards the bathroom door ending in a pointed finger.

"Oh, hello, Joe," Ashley said completely ignoring his question, and continuing to apply her mascara. "How are you? How was your trip? How's the new girlfriend? Had a fun filled few days after dumping your family Joe?" Ashley's sarcasm couldn't be contained.

"Ashley, stop acting like Madison, and answer me," Joe demanded, and reworded his question. "Why have I returned from New York to find your parents camped out in my guest room?" Joe said, his fury escalating.

Ashley began her monologue, "Well, let me seeeeee JOE. First, of all that is OUR guestroom, and oh, yes, maybe they're here because you abandoned THEIR DAUGHTER on Independence Day at the West Palm Beach airport to go off to NEW YORK, to join your NEW girlfriend, and celebrate Independence day with her, who probably has NO children of her own. Your wife gets drunk because she is so devastated. Because she always TRUSTED YOU, and because she was really supposed to be having a wonderful fun-filled day with HER husband and children at a friends house party. Oh, yes and then your wife's Independence Day celebration Joe, ended up in the West Palm Beach COUNTY JAIL JOE, AND THE PARTY AT THE WEST PALM BEACH JAIL WAS SO INTOXICATING JOE, THAT SHE HAD TO BE BROUGHT HOME BY A TAXI JOE, AFTERALL HER CAR WAS IMPOUNDED FROM THE FIRST INTOXICATING PARTY SHE HAD, HAD THAT VERY SAME DAY JOE!!!!" Ashley was red in the face, and again on the verge of tears. Then much more calmly, because she felt like she had no more energy left in her, she said, "You see the one acting like Madison here, Joe, IS YOU!" Ashley turned back to the mirror.

"Oh, I'm sorry Ash. Why didn't you call and tell me. I would have helped you," Joe said genuinely concerned.

"Oh, my G-d!" said Ashley, completely frustrated and turning back to face Joe. "Is there no end to your STUPIDITY? Why would I call you Joe, when you had just left me for another woman Joe? Do you think I am that lame, that desperate, that sad? Do you Joe? Well, do you? I would rather call the 1-800-EVANGELICAL hotline THAN CALL YOU!" Ashley ended yelling again. She turned back to the mirror, shaking with frustration, desperation and rage. What planet does this guy live on? Ashley thought now becoming hysterical.

"Well, it just feels uncomfortable with them here while we are going through all of this stuff. Can't you send them home at least until we have worked through all of it?" Joe said much more quietly, and still puzzled as to how so much 'had' actually happened in the few days he was away.

"No," said Ashley, "it's you that has to be sent away Joe, not them. So, all your stuff is packed in boxes in the garage. I strongly suggest you find somewhere else to sleep tonight, and every night from hereon out. Oh, and kindly call me so we can arrange for the children to see you. I don't want you coming around whenever you want to anymore," Ashley instructed Joe. She had discovered this tactic from bits of information she had gathered, or thought she gathered from a program on television discussing, "How to get Divorced, the Peaceful Way." It was hosted by a lawyer who had been practicing Family Law for years.

"You packed all my stuff in boxes?" Joe questioned like he had been wounded.

He had seen the boxes when he returned and walked through the garage, but it didn't phase him. Ashley was often stacking up boxes in the garage as she redecorated rooms.

"What happened to the 'our' you mentioned a moment ago? If this is *our* guestroom then this is still *our* house," Joe continued. But Joe knew that was not what she had meant earlier.

"My baseball collection?" he asked.

"In the boxes," Ashley responded.

"My comic collection?"

"In the boxes," Ashley repeated.

"What about my Hugo Boss suits?"

"In the boxes!" Ashley yelled frustrated, "everything is in the boxes Joe. Now I suggest you leave," she ended curtly.

"I guess this is it," Joe said.

Ashley was unsure whether this was meant to be a question or statement but she responded anyway, "Yes, Joe, thanks to you, this is it!"

"I'm going to see the children. I've missed them," said Joe, leaving the bathroom.

Ashley dropped down onto the bathroom stool next to her. She was in shock, and terribly upset. The tears began to roll off her cheeks like a vast river which had been split into two continuous streams. The salt water removed everything, washing it down Ashley's face onto her lap, eyeliner, mascara, base, everything was being washed away. He misses the children, but he never missed me, she thought to herself. Ashley pulled a number of tissues out of the tissue box to wipe her face. She looked down at the crumpled bunch of tissues in her hand. All that mascara, she thought, I really must start to buy waterproof mascara, especially if this divorce is going to make me cry so much!

∞∞∞

For two days after Ashley had returned home from the county jail she cried. She never left her room. She took no calls, except one from her mother. She barely ate, and she barely saw the children. She couldn't face leaving her room. God had won. He had finally won and destroyed her completely. She was no match for him, she had decided.

First, David's father Joshua and now Joe. What is it with these names that begin with 'J?' One thing was for sure, she told herself, I will marry no more 'J' names. J, she thought stands for Junk. That's it. Junk. Why didn't God tell her this before? Why did she have to work it all out by herself?

Her phone beeped a musical note. This usually meant she had a voice message waiting. Let me guess, she said to herself, Joe's plane crashed, I need to identify the body, a cute friend of his will meet me at the airport to comfort me, he left a fat insurance policy for me to collect on, and his girlfriend is left crying hysterically in her apartment, her private Independence Day dinner she had planned with Joe sitting on the table, ruined. Yip, sounds about right! A smile formed on her lips. She scooped up her phone with gusto from the bedside table, pressed the appropriate buttons, and listened to her voice mail, hoping… hoping…

"Hi, Ash it's Pam."

I know who you are! Thought Ashley annoyed. Why do people say that, it's so annoying, hi it's me! She said mockingly.

"Haven't heard from you since you left my house on Independence Day. Is everything okay? Saw the cutest chick flick, and Amber said she would lend me the book to read. Oh, yeah, and Amber took me to see Brianna's new blue shoes. You know the ones you saw on Saturday night at *Aqua's*? To die for, Ash! I can't believe you never told me about them. Oh, I'm on the website right now trying to order a pair for myself. Totally love them!!! Dying to go for a mani and pedi with you. Call me."

Ashley threw her phone away to the far end of the bed, arched her back and head, and let out a deafening scream. She held it for as long as her lungs would allow, then collapsed back into the bed's mattress. It was so loud that it caused Nina to knock on her door and ask if everything was alright.

"Yes, I'm fine, thank you, Nina." She had responded sweetly.

And then she started to giggle. She must sound like one of those loony females having a mental breakdown behind closed doors like in Jane Eyre. She had just seen its re-release at the movies. Now why don't I have an Edward Rochester? She thought dreamily. Oh, of course because his name begins with an 'E,' and stupid Ashley here only goes for the letter 'J!'

"Is there any end to those fucking blue shoes?" She said aloud, "That bitch. I've still got to get her back."

But right now Ashley had bigger fish to fry – Joe. Her thoughts were erratic. A mani and pedi? My life is in the toilet, and she wants me to go out and have a mani and pedi with her! Sure Pam what else is there to do with my life? And enjoy your visit to see the *blue shoes*. MY stolen blue shoes!!

"And that reminds me," she said out loud, picking up her phone from the edge of the bed.

Ashley went into her contacts, found Joe's name and number and changed his name from Joe to "Lying Cheating Pig." Great she thought. So every time he called she would be encouraged by those words as they revealed themselves on her incoming phone screen. Perfect. Good luck to whatever-your-name-is girlfriend!!

When Ashley got back from jail, Nina who had taken over from Olivia, told the children their mother was sick, and needed to be alone in bed to recover, and not to go in or they would get sick too.

Amber wanted to know if it was a "big people's sick?"

Nina smiling answered, 'Yes.'

"Then why can't I go in and see Mommy, if it's a big people's sick, I'm a kid I can't get sick?" Amber pushed the subject.

"Nice try," Nina responded, cradling Amber in her arms and swinging her around making her squeal, and laugh in delight. Anything, which would help her forget her concern over her mother.

David, who obviously wasn't buying into it, being a few years older than the other two, sneaked into his mother's room the next afternoon, after day camp. He had heard her crying hysterically behind her closed bedroom door several times the night before. He sneaked in when the sitter wasn't looking, and went to sit next to his mother on the bed. She was curled up in a ball under the covers sniffling.

"Mom," he said, "I know something is wrong why don't you just tell me? I can help you. I don't like to see you so sad. Where were you? I was scared. Dad called and I had to make up some weird excuse because he wanted to speak to you, and I didn't know where you were. We called you so many times. Please tell me, what's wrong Mom?" David pleaded sweetly.

Ashley stopped sniffling. She threw off the covers. "How did you get in here?" she said, eyes red and puffy, holding a tissue in her one hand and a bunch of tissues in the other.

"I just walked in through the door. Mom, it's ok, it's me. Please tell me what's wrong?" David kept pressing. "Amber and Joe Jr keep crying. They want to come in and see you. Nina keeps telling them you're sick," David continued, concerned.

Ashley pulled the covers back over her head, curled up again, and said, "Well, I am sick. Sick and tired," she said, and began to cry again.

"Well, I can't do anything if you don't tell me what's wrong. I'm going over to Ari. She lives in Oxford Park. I'll ride my bike over there," David said, not wanting to push his mother anymore, "I have my cell."

Ashley popped her head out from under the covers, "You really like this Ari, don't you David? You talk about her all the time," Ashley asked.

David rolled his eyes back, "Yes, Mom I like Ari. She's pretty and she makes me laugh. We have all the same friends."

"That's nice, honey," Ashley responded, "I know it's only July but do you want to ask her to join us when we go to *Jingle Ball* in December? I have an extra ticket. Pappy and Gran will be here." Giving Joe's ticket away brought her great joy.

"Yeah!" David responded his eyes wide with excitement. He knew the *Jingle Ball* line up was going to be awesome this year, and Ari loved so many of the artists who would be performing. "Can I go now?" David asked, returning to his usual pre-teen age, and dying to break the news to Ari.

"Of course. And, thanks for coming to see me David. I really appreciate it."

"Fine," David said impatiently, long passed his concern over his mother, and set off.

After David's visit Ashley began to feel a little better. He seemed to have left her with a brighter energy. How she loved his caring heart. She got up and pulled back the shades revealing the full frequency spectrum of the Florida sun. She picked up the remote on the dresser and clicked on the afternoon television shows.

"You have been married a long time now, what twelve or fourteen years? And how is your marriage with Ron going?" asked the interviewer on a popular afternoon channel.

"Oh, we have the most wonderful marriage. We can read one another's thoughts. He is so thoughtful, buys me flowers all the time and writes me love notes, and.."

"Blah, blah, blah, blah…and you make me sick!" Ashley droned over the voice of the guest on the show, and changed channels.

She found an old time favorite of hers, *Little house on the Prairie*. She continued to watch, sinking back into bed, and enjoying the calm rhythm of the show. So, much better she thought than goody Miss Two Shoes, and her f'ing mind blowing marriage!

Ashley was grateful her parents arrived as promised. She couldn't face being a mother at this point in time in her life. Her father was able to retrieve her impounded car, and her mother took over, instructing, directing and turning her household into a well-oiled machine. She cooked scrumptious meals, and soon Ashley felt loved again. She brought Ashley a mound of mail and sat besides her as she sorted through it all. She created a pile for bills, a pile for household improvements, a pile of junk mail, and a pile for lawyers, criminal lawyers.

"I better find a lawyer to deal with those idiots down at that courthouse. I think I will give this one a call today Mom, and make an appointment," She said to her mother pointing to the advertisement she liked. The only one advertisement she received depicting a female criminal lawyer.

"Are you feeling up to all that, Darling?" asked her mother.

"No Mom. But I don't think I will ever feel up to it. I just have no choice. I have to do it. And I hope it doesn't mess up my divorce, " Ashley answered.

Ashley scheduled her first criminal lawyer's appointment the next morning at eleven thirty. The only lawyers she had ever met formally was the one who drafted their wills, when Amber was born, and the one, who had transferred the title of their house when they bought it four years ago. Both appointments seemed pretty mundane, and the wills lawyer was so unexciting he sounded like he was reading from a script as he asked every question under the sun to decide the best way to set out their wills. Joe was concerned that if both of them died the children should be raised by his mother. Ashley didn't mind, although her parents were a little upset.

"It doesn't mean you won't see them Mom. I'll be sure to see to that. But anyway, we're not going to die any time soon. It's like Grandma always used to say, only the good die young," Ashley had tried to lighten the mood.

After these past few days, she was definitely going to change her will to read that her parents were to take the children in should they both die. But she really didn't have any great urgency to change her will, she thought again, with the kind of track record Joe has right now, he'll live well into his nineties!

Chapter FIVE

"If you have any court papers Mrs. Loveit, please bring those in too. And, don't forget all the jail papers. Did they take your driver's license away?" asked the lawyer's secretary.

"Yes, they did," Ashley answered in a mocking sing-a-long tone as she once again mentally recalled her debut, and final appearances before the jail clerk.

"Well, please be sure you get a ride here or take a taxi. Look forward to meeting you tomorrow Mrs. Loveit. Thank you for calling." And that was it. Click. Call over.

That wasn't too bad now was it Ashley? She thought to herself, proudly. She had made the call she said she would. I think I will even go downstairs for dinner tonight. I've missed the kids.

And that's how Ashley finally got herself out of her bedroom. One call to the criminal lawyer was all it took. The next morning she washed her hair, blow dried and straightened it. She chose to wear the most formal pinstriped suit she owned, complimented by a perfectly crisp laundered white shirt, Nina had recently picked up from the cleaners. She had to look like an educated, affluent, and totally together mother. Anything, but some drunken, lost, and helpless female, no doubt Officer End and his buddies would say she was, before that grumpy old judge in court.

She would show them. She would show up looking like a million dollars. That will fix them all. Make them eat their words. They will be begging for forgiveness, and Ashley decided she would turn up her nose and walk away. Just like that, and she snapped her fingers to emphasize her point.

Ashley's lawyer didn't quite look like the photo in her advertisement. She was much more mature looking, and her trouser suit seemed a little more shabby. But then nor did her secretary Candice, match up to her sweet, concerned telephone voice, either, but Ashley brushed all this aside. After all, it's not about what they look like now, is it?

She completed the form she was given by Candice in the waiting room, and didn't wait long, before being called into Marge Win's office. Marge had graduated from law school about twenty years earlier. She had a husband, two children, both girls, and she lived in a neighborhood in the county south of Ashley's.

"It's very nice to meet you Mrs. Loveit," Marge said, shaking Ashley's hand.

Marge and Candice had met many Ashley's over the years. They would come in all cleaned up, looking like the sweet, perfect wife, and mother, and profess their undying upright citizenship lifestyle. Invariably, breaking down into tears in Marge's office or later with Candice in her office over the smallest of 'potential' outcomes Marge may have mentioned in their case. Marge felt she was not doing her job properly if she didn't make her clients aware of 'potential' outcomes in their cases, because she couldn't risk any wild hysteria before any judge or jury. And these women were notorious for their outbursts of morality in the courtroom before any judge who showed them even the slightest notion they would lend them a tiny, tiny, tiny ear. And besides, this was what her clients were paying her for, her years of knowledge in the court system. Well, that's how Marge understood it, perhaps not the Ashley's of the world, but definitely the Marge's.

These woman, she had noticed were quick to hire her because she naturally gave off a very warm, nurturing and to the point attitude. Many of them, Marge also realized, needed a male energy disguised as a mother figure, who would be able to instruct them on what to do. Marge often fit this bill too. She easily stood up to any tough opposing male counsel. In fact, she welcomed it.

Her most memorable times with these types of clients was always when she received a copy of the sheriff's video tape recordings taken on the night of the DUI investigation. In an instant all their firm beliefs like, 'they have mixed up the police report that wasn't me' or 'I wasn't drunk' or 'they treated me so badly,' would melt away as she and her client would view the video recording together. Her best was when they claimed they had absolutely refused to take the breathalyzer test, and there they would be in full view of the camera making endless attempts at trying to blow into the breathalyzer tubes with the sheriff's technician avidly docketing the level of alcohol in their bloodstream, with each blow of air they made into the tube.

"You do understand that if you wish to fight your case, this video will be shown in court to the jury? And if it is shown to the jury, you're probably going to loose right there on the spot," Marge would point out.

Then came the moment of truth, the reason why they were invariably in this situation from the start; an affair, a deserting husband, a secret drinking addiction, depression. The list was endless. Sometimes Marge, and many times even Candice, would have to counsel these clients far more than any others. They were full of baggage.

But they loved to bestow gifts. In appreciation for the slightest compassion extended by you they would pop up at the most unusual times of day with handfuls of goodies they had seen at some store or another, which had triggered a thought of no one other than their beloved lawyer and her assistant.

However, there was often an ulterior motive attached to their huge generosity: These women were trying to bribe you to keep your mouth shut never to disclose what you had read on their police reports or seen on the video tape. They so struggled with the concept of attorney-client privilege, no matter how many times you emphasized it. Possibly because Marge believed, they lived in a world of permanent gossip and knew only too well what could happen if any of 'this stuff' got out.

They would be ecstatic when you offered them the video for their own keeping at the end of the case, having no understanding of the concept that it was a copy, and the original lay in the archives at the sheriff's office. They also didn't seem to comprehend the fact that their charges were for public viewing online, and their files available at the courthouse upon request. They were all so fragile.

They would always remind her of the Coldplay song, "Lost." *Just because you are a big fish in a little pond doesn't mean you won, because there will only come along a bigger one.* In their case, that big one was the State of Florida. That was the part of the cycle of life they never seemed to anticipate.

Marge wasted no time in getting down to business with Ashley. Something Ashley appreciated, because although she felt she looked the part, she acknowledged the fact she was still feeling rather vulnerable inside, after days of lying in bed tucked away from the workings of the world.

"May I take a look at that paper you received in court please Mrs. Loveit?"

"Oh, sure. And please call me Ashley," Ashley responded passing Marge the paper, and then nestling primly back into her chair, feeling proud about how she looked.

Marge buzzed through to Candice, "Candice can you come in here a moment please." Moments later Candice knocked on the door.

"Candice will you please just run this case number, and see if any court date has been set for Mrs Loveit yet, and if so at which county courthouse? Thanks Candice." Candice nodded and was gone in an instant.

"I think it is too early for a court date yet, but we should check anyway, because you never know with 'this' clerk's office. They can always surprise you," Marge continued aimlessly.

"Don't you want to hear what happened, and how awful those officers treated me, and as for the people at the jail, well they …." Ashley began without being prompted.

Marge put a hand up as if stopping traffic, "Please Ashley, let me ask you the questions first. I promise you'll have a chance to tell me everything."

Ashley took off on a mental tangent: I'm not sure if I chose the right lawyer. If she won't listen to me like those ones in court then who will? But wait a minute, that's what that woman said to me in court, get yourself a lawyer because these ones here they only talk to others that are the same as them. Ashley felt better again about her choice. Look at that sweet picture with her two little girls. Ashley automatically assumed the two girls in the photo holder directly behind Marge were hers.

Looking down at Ashley's court papers Marge began, "Well, it looks like Ashley, you were arrested, and then charged with two criminal charges, one for Reckless driving and one for DUI. Now you need to understand something, DUI is looked upon quite seriously in Florida, and the DMV, the Department of Motor Vehicles, operates separately from the court system, and can still take away your driver's license for six months if they feel they have cause to. And this DUI will remain on your driver's record for another several decades. It can also cause your auto insurance to go up." This was not quite the news Ashley was hoping for.

Candice interrupted with the information Marge had asked for, and Marge shared it with Ashley.

"Well, it is as I expected. While your charges are set, a court date has not been. That will come later in a couple of weeks by mail to your home, unless you of course have retained me to be your lawyer. That way all correspondence which comes from the courts, the state prosecutor, and DMV will come directly to me. Makes it a little easier, and much less overwhelming for you."

Wow, there was so much information, Ashley thought. Charges, DMV, court dates, my head is spinning. Thanks Joe, Ashley thought, her victimhood status rearing its head again.

"Now," Marge continued to explain, "a lot depends on whether you choose to fight these charges or not. And let me be quite clear about this Ashley. Unless there is some chance I think you can win from looking at all the evidence, it could be a lost cause. Then we need to look into entering a plea bargain with the state prosecutor, so we can avoid you doing jail time."

"Jail time!!" Ashley bolted upright in her chair, "I absolutely refuse to do jail time! Those officers bullied me into leaving my car. They were abusive, rude, and at that jail they were not any better…"

Again Marge's hand went up, "Ashley, please I understand how terribly upset you are, but…" before Marge could get the next word out, Ashley was sobbing.

"You don't understand what has happened to my life. My whole life is collapsing, I've been crying for days in my room, I haven't seen my kids, my parents had to come down to be with me, my husband's divorcing me. Someone stole my blue shoes. I'm just left, abandoned, like a piece of old butcher meat," Ashley wasn't sure where the 'old butcher meat' part came in but it just spewed out of her mouth.

"Here," said Marge passing Ashley a tissue box. Marge had a fixed weekly order for tissues on the office supply list Candice took to Office Mart.

"I'm sorry to hear that Ashley. But honey, the judge and state prosecutor you need to understand will not care. In fact they don't care about your life's issues. They have a job to do, and that is to keep drunk drivers off the Florida roads as much as possible to save lives. If they are easy on you then you may not heed to their warning, and just go out, and get drunk again, and the next time injure or even kill someone. Okay? You have to try and take this all a little less personally," Marge said.

"How can I take it less personally? It's my life. It *is* personal!" Ashley blurted out, although she did feel a smidge less broken by what Marge had just said.

"How much does it cost to hire you?" asked Ashley out of the blue.

Marge buzzed Candice again, "Candice, can you please draft up a contract for Mrs. Loveit, and bring it in to me. Thanks."

Ashley felt a little better. Marge Wins wanted *her* as a client. She started to breath a little easier.

As promised earlier Marge addressed Ashley, "Now, Ashley, why don't you tell me what happened on Independence Day?"

Ashley sat upright in her chair again, and began her long saga from the point where she had made plans to go over to Pam's that day. Marge listened patiently to her life long animated narrative, interrupting now and again to ask those *legal* questions lawyers need to ask. She took down very few notes while Ashley conveyed her very, very long tale, because for Marge most of what Ashley was saying was largely superfluous with regards to her case, and purely Ashley's personal opinions of people and events, which Marge found quite entertaining, especially the part about the inmates cat calling. She was very familiar with the prisoner's behavior of that jail building because the courthouse, like the jail holding cells where Ashley was held, is also located right next door, and Marge herself had fallen victim to the 'all male' chorus many a time.

Marge let Ashley continue also because she could clearly see it was having a positive affect in clearing up her tearful frame of mind.

At the end of her story, Ashley said, "So, do you think I have enough evidence to get the case dismissed?"

Marge couldn't help but burst out laughing, "I'm sorry," she said to a rather puzzled Ashley.

"Ashley, I will need to see exactly what those officers have written in their reports about you, and see what is in the court file before I can give any kind of an evaluation on your case," she continued, "you need to understand that whatever story you have told me here today will be a complete 180 from the details entered by those officers in the police report."

"You mean they going to lie?" Ashley said shocked.

"No, Ashley, it means they interpreted things differently than you. I've read literally hundreds of these reports. They will probably say they saw someone who showed signs of driving recklessly, and so pulled you over. They will probably then go on to say that there were more signs that you had been drinking and so they stopped you driving. They have rules and procedures which they have to follow. Now from what you just told me, and understand everything you do tell me remains in this room forever, you had been drinking. But I need to see how the officers proceeded in carrying out their rules, and exactly what they say happened. You will also be happy to know you will be assigned a new Judge. The first one you saw is what they called your First Appearance Judge. Once your case is assigned to a courtroom it will be re-assigned a new Judge."

That was certainly good news for Ashley, "Oh great," she said.

"But," continued Marge, there always seemed to be a 'but' when it came to Marge, "this new judge may not necessarily be a better one, he or she could be one that takes a very hard core approach to DUI's, or could be a judge who is a little more lenient on first time offenders. We won't know who the judge is for a few weeks yet."

Ashley wrote out a check retaining Marge for her legal services right then and there. She wasn't going to take any chances after everything she had heard that morning. She didn't want to be dealing alone with any more of those grumpy judges, and besides Marge promised her as she took her retainer, that from this point on she would not have to be alone before any criminal law judge again.

Ashley left Marge Win's office feeling much better, well, better in some way, but her life was still a mess. And it was about to get messier.

∞∞∞

Joe felt very uncomfortable having to sit with his children at the kitchen table as they nibbled on some cheese and crackers, after arguing with Ashley in the bathroom. Sitting alongside Joe, Jr. and Madison were his in-laws, one at either end of the rectangular table. Usually Ashley's Mom would be cooking up a storm in the kitchen, and chatting away about her organic garden and new hybrid flowers she had recently encountered at the local organic market.

Today, all she said was, "hello, Joe." And, it wasn't a friendly "hello, Joe, nice to see you again Joe," either. Rather, it was a "hello, Joe, what the hell are you doing with your life, and my daughter's, Joe!"

Joe, Jr. articulated the tension all so beautifully when he innocently asked, "So, where have you been Daddy? Did you have fun?" Joe looked at Joe Jr.

"I had to go to New York, Joe," his father responded.

"Oh, cool," said Joe Jr. excitedly, "Mom's favorite city," he added.

The tension remained at a peak as Joe Jr. asked his father a follow up question. "Gran and I have been painting Daddy. Do you want to see what I painted? It's a clown, Daddy. A sad clown with a happy face. See Mommy was crying, and it made me sad, but I didn't want the clown to have a sad face because I wanted Mommy to smile again so I painted a happy clown. Do you want to see it Daddy?" Joe, Jr. urged tugging at his father's shirt sleeve.

"Please Daddy, please, please…" he begged.

Joe felt sick, and swallowed hard. He didn't realize how easily the children could be affected by all of this. At that moment his cell phone rang in his top shirt pocket. Both in-laws starred at him….watching…waiting…for him to pick it up. He slowly pulled it out his pocket and silenced the ringer.

"Aren't you going to answer your phone, Daddy? You always answer your phone," asked Joe, Jr. Again, innocently creating even more tension, if this was even possible at that point, thought Joe.

"No, thanks Joe it can wait. I'm here to see how you guys are doing," Joe responded outwardly as calmly as he could.

"Pappy has been taking me to school and picking me up. We have so much fun. One time he picked me up, and we went to that ice-cream store, you know the one that has ice cream that comes out the wall? Then we got lots of M & M's to put on our ice cream like sprinkles. And Gran cooks such nice food. Mmmmm…Don't tell mom I said that," Joe, Jr. said giggling holding his hand over his mouth as if hiding his laughter from someone.

He had always been a bit like Ashley Joe thought. Never lost for conversation. Joe felt a little sad. Why would he want to leave all of this? He wondered.

Joe addressed his in-laws, "Do you mind if I could have a little time with them," he said indicating the children, "I need to talk to them."

Ashley's parents looked at one another, then Ashley's mother said, "sure, we can move. We were hoping to take a walk around the Woodfield circle anyway, perhaps now would be a good time."

"Thank you," Joe said.

Madison had been very quiet since Joe had arrived. She continued to play with all the little people she had placed around the table in front of her.

"I have something to tell you both. You need to listen to me. Madison? Please listen to Daddy," Joe urged looking at her.

Madison stopped for a moment, holding one of her little people in her small hand and said, "Yes, Daddy."

"Daddy, is going to move to a new house. Mommy is going to stay in this house with you both. But you will still get to see me. You will get to visit me in my new house," he waited for the children to respond.

"Can David come too?" asked Madison.

"Of course he can if he wants to," Joe said.

"Will you have a swimming pool Daddy?" Joe Jr. asked.

"Would you like that Joe, if I had a swimming pool?" responded Joe.

"Yes! Yes! Yes!" Joe Jr. exclaimed exploding with excitement, and making Joe feel a little more at ease. Joe sat around with the kids a little longer, until Olivia arrived, and he told them he had to go and look for the new house he promised them.

"Livvy, Livvy," Joe Jr. called. He struggled to pronounce Olivia's name. "Daddy's going to get a new house and we are all invited!"

Olivia raised both her eyebrows, and all she said was, "that's nice Joe."

Joe began to pack some of his boxes into his car. His car was a coupe and so he could only fit a few boxes in the trunk and on the back seat. He would have to make a few trips.

David saw him packing in the garage. He had stopped by the house to pick up his iPod and a few other things he wanted to use at his friend's house. On his way out of the house David went up to Joe in the garage.

"You leaving, you just got back?" David said, beginning to tear up a little.

"Oh. Hi, David. Yes. It is best if your mother and I split up for a while. When I get a place you can visit though, with Madison and Joe, Jr. if you like."

"But we were all so happy. Why are you doing this? We were all a family again," David began to cry openly. He was desperate for a family, any family which made him feel whole.

"I'm sorry David things happen in life, and sometimes they're hard to explain to children. One day you will understand. You're in charge now. You're the eldest. So be sure to look after your siblings, and your mom."

David walked away feeling completely hollow and conquered. Shortly afterwards, Joe reversed out of the driveway. As he passed David and Ari on the street, he saw Ari put her arm around him, comforting him, in his rearview mirror. Joe didn't feel too sad.

At the first stop sign he pulled out his cell phone, highlighted his mother's name in his contact list, and his phone did the rest. His mother lived in Broward County just south of them. She had a good size home on one of the large water canals, with a detached guest house. "Hi, Mom, it's Joe, listen I need to stay with you for a few days. Will that be okay?"

"Sure Joe," said his mother, "Is everything okay?" she asked.

"Yes, Mom, everything is fine. I'll fill you in when I see you."

He then called Mel, "Hi, baby, I miss you," and before Mel could respond he continued, "Well, you will be happy to know, Ashley threw me out! She had all my stuff packed in boxes when I got back. All I had to do was pack them in the car and I was out of there! Tell me what you wearing. I've been thinking of those little green shorts you had on last night all day today…" and so Joe's conversation went.

∞∞

It had been four days since Ashley had retained Marge as her lawyer. Marge had called her to begin the process to apply for a limited driver's license from DMV so she could take the children to and from school, and to go to the neighborhood store to purchase supplies. In the meantime, Nina helped her out. She told Nina she had to take a special medication and couldn't tell the children, but one of the side affects was very strong and she couldn't drive yet. It would take a little while before she got used to the medication. Ashley felt comfortable that Nina wouldn't say anything if she knew the truth, but Ashley wasn't going to risk any 'slip of the tongue,' incidents.

Ashley also heard one other time from Marge when she told her that she had filed a Notice of Appearance with the Courts, to inform the Clerk of Court Marge was now representing Ashley, and all court correspondence was to go directly to her, and not Ashley. At that point Marge told Ashley not to expect to hear from her for a few weeks because the process took some time to infiltrate the criminal court system.

In the meantime, Ashley tried desperately to get back into routine with the children. Her parents thought it best they return home, and Ashley look into getting a divorce lawyer. 'That' was something Ashley was struggling with. She just couldn't get herself to make the call.

Ashley's phone rang and, 'Lying Cheating Pig' came up on Ashley's screen. Joe asked if he could have the kids sleep over the next day. Ashley agreed, and made sure Nina remembered to pack Madison's float jacket for the pool. And once again, as was the case with Olivia, Nina responded with irritation that she had remembered to include the swim jacket. David asked to sleep out at a friend's house after summer camp that day, he wasn't ready to spend time alone with Joe, and so

Joe picked up the other two kids at two in the afternoon as planned. Right after Joe picked up the kids, and as if tracking her thoughts, Pam called.

"Hi, Ash. You got plans for tonight? Where have you been, I haven't heard from you in ages? I thought I was going to get your voice message again," asked Pam.

"I've been sick. But no I don't have plans. What are you doing?" Ashley responded.

"Oh, we thought a light Thai dinner and a movie. Girls night. Interested?"

"Who's going?" Ashley asked.

"Me, Amber, and Taylor," strange Pam thought, Ashley never asks whose going.

"You know Taylor was asking after you. She's got a new boyfriend. She told me to call and ask you to join us. So, like, HERE I AM calling!" Pam ended in her usual high pitch squeal as if she was still in high school.

The doorbell rang. A perfect excuse to get off the phone, "I've got to go Pam there's someone at the door."

Ashley opened the door without even questioning who was out there. After all, it was Woodfield, she looked out the front door sidelights to see who was knocking. Funny she hadn't called anyone through the gate today, maybe it was a neighbor.

"Mrs. Ashley Loveit?" asked a young man dressed in blue jeans and a t-shirt. Usually someone dressed in denim jeans and a t-shirt at her front door was there to deliver a bouquet of flowers from the florist, but there were no flowers in sight.

"Yes," said Ashley.

"This is for you Ma'am." And before she could respond he had dumped a pile of papers in her hands.

"Consider yourself served. Have a nice day."

Ashley stood there, taken aback. She looked down at her hands. All she took in was a caption that read: Notice of Filing for Dissolution of Marriage.

She closed the front door and walked numbly over to the half moon couch. The house was quiet. She sat down at the edge of the couch and balanced the papers on her lap. Her heart was pounding. Ashley suddenly realized why Joe had been so insistent on an exact time to pick up the kids, he was never that particular, and he knew she hadn't changed the secret code to let a guest through the gate at Woodfield. The process server cannot get in unless someone from the household had called for clearance. Only she and Joe knew the code to clear someone through the gate. He had planned it perfectly. A total jerk she had married, a total jerk. He could have called her, and told her he had gone to see a lawyer and was starting the proceedings. He didn't have to do it this way.

Then she continued as all Woodfield women did, look for the female to blame to excuse the male from any wrong doing or part in any scheme. Of course, he's staying with his mother!

Joe's mother had always had an issue with Ashley. She watched everything she did, and constantly criticized her to Joe behind her back. She knew, because Joe would tell her. But then when Ashley had her boobs done, so did Joe's mother. When Ashley had her lips pumped, so did Joe's mother. When Ashley had lipo so did his mother. The list went on and on. She even copied Ashley's living room drapes. Pam told her for years Joe's mother secretly wanted to be her, but Ashley thought Pam was just being her normal *bitchy* self.

Ashley picked up her cell phone and called Pam back. She was unusually calm after receiving such a shock. She also realized a frolicsome evening would do her good. With that kind of combination of girls going out, there would be little need for her to even talk much, just listen and laugh, largely at them, for a change.

"Listen Pam, what time did you say you wanted to go out tonight?"

"Well, around seven thirty Ash. Why?" Pam asked.

"Can you pick me up? I'm not in the mood to drive," Ashley asked.

"Absolutely!" Pam responded, "anything for my *best* friend."

"Yeah, right," Ashley responded remembering high school and the boy's locker room. "Thanks see you later," said Ashley.

Okay Joe strike one for you.

However, what Joe didn't know was the Ashley he knew, the one he had hoodwinked for all these years, was beginning to fade, in more ways than one.

Chapter SIX

F or centuries authors, poets, song writers, and other artists have developed the concept of the rose thorn. In *The Nightingale and the Rose* by Oscar Wilde, a bird bent on bestowing a red rose to the one he loves allows his heart to be pierced by a rose thorn, its trickle of blood magically turning a white flowering rose into a red one. But for those who study plants, the Rose bush doesn't contain thorns at all, rather prickles. And therefore, Botanist's like Brian Capon define rose prickles as "woody epidermal outgrowths growing randomly" along the stem between the bud nodes. A more perfect description of Lily could not be found anywhere else. Lily White was a random outgrowth who lived in Woodfield Suburban Club.

Just as, many prickles on a rose bush are curved downward to deter predators from climbing upwards, so Lily would reveal another side to life, one which would relieve countless women from life's predators, even though many of those predators were mostly traits within themselves. And, during this process of growth, came the birth of the ultimate realization that 'they' needed to get out of their own way in order to grow. And so it was Lily who provided a soft landing along the way to lessen the pain and anguish they would feel during their rebirth.

Lily White's soft landing was for those who sought her out. People, she believed God placed in her path in this lifetime, to bleed deeper meaning into their frail existence, or rather return them to their true selves as loving caring Souls. The Rose ironically is often referred to as the flower of transformation, an unknown fact among the Woodfield women. None-the-less, they all went through it, those who chose to be connected to Lily that is, after the apocalypse would always follow the epiphany, and sometimes there were many of them.

There was one more thing about Lily. All the advice she gave to help others she firmly believed was from another source, a source much higher than herself, one which was Divinely inspired to do good, and spread light across the world. She was merely a messenger, and therefore wouldn't take any credit for any good she did. When something she said helped a person turn their life around, she would tell them modestly, "I am merely the channel. You took the hardest step, you chose to get on the train, wherever it takes you is unimportant once you are aware of the powers of the Universe." She always used the words Universe and God interchangeably because some felt comfortable with the use of the word God, others not.

Lily first truly understood her mission in Woodfield when Sandy, a mother of one of her daughter's friends, sought her out because she had heard Lily was a spiritual medium. Both Lily's grandfather and father had been natural mediums, and Lily was the third generation. A spiritual medium on Sandy's doorstep proved very convenient, she could make a quick stop amid the hair and nail salon. Sandy had lost a sister who was particularly close to her. She felt her sister was desperately trying to reach her from the other side, but Sandy couldn't disclose this to her husband. She explained this to Lily by mentioning a series of light bulbs which would continually go out when just recently replaced by her, and other things which seemed to have moved after she had placed them in a particular spot. Or when books her sister used to love reading fell off the bookshelves when no one was around. Sandy's husband was a renowned local heart surgeon, and not into any of this 'woo-woo' stuff, and therefore she was very insistent Lily not breathe a word of their meeting to anyone. Lily, while not quite sure who she would reveal their meeting to, or who would even have the remotest interest in hearing the details, promised Sandy anyway.

Lily told Sandy she did not go out of her way to be contacted by the other side, but if you sat in a session with her, and there was a relative or friend who wanted to make contact with their Earth connections she would provide the means, as long as the energies on the other side were not mischievous, and serious about helping those left behind. Lily did not always remember what she said during a session. Mostly because the information would travel right through her, but her clients invariably always helped her to restore her memory with tidbits of their sessions. What was natural for Lily during these sessions, was clearly a fascination for the Woodfield women.

"I know that was her!" Sandy said with delight after the session, her enormous boobs stood straight out barely moving even though the rest of her body was gyrating. Sandy had recently had massive oversized breast implants.

"Those are the exact words she would use when she was alive: He's no good for you, he is causing you way too much pain, he's cheating on you, just leave him."

It always amazed Lily how it was the most simple words and phrases which helped her clients find comfort, and how those few words were enough for them to clearly identify their loved ones. Another thing that surprised Lily, was how few of them heeded to the warnings they were given. They would revel more in the fact they had identified their loved ones on the other side, than listening to the value of the message being relayed.

And it was written in the stars Ashley was soon to meet Lily, as she too would need a soft place to land.

∞∞∞

Ashley hired a divorce lawyer, a lawyer recommended by the only other lawyer she knew, Marge. Renee Parker, was very compassionate, and during those early days, was the kind of lawyer Ashley needed. As time went on, however, Ashley found Renee far too compassionate. She became much too empathetic with Joe's legal position, even though it was Ashley who had stressed she wanted a peaceful divorce.

When Ashley labeled Joe's approach to gain primary guardianship of their children "a fake ploy by his mother to use the kids to get back at her," Renee felt he was just exploring all his options, and it wasn't unusual to see this kind of a demand in a legal notice of marriage dissolution. Usual or not, Ashley deemed the mere fact Florida had no laws identifying infidelity in a marriage as a reason to have all her demands met she decided to even the score herself, by being sure she created as many hoops, loops and obstacles as she so desired to mend her broken heart. Let the girlfriend know, she was not going to have any sweet walkover ex-wife lingering around. So, Ashley would find legitimate excuses, like having to take the children for their annual shots, to delay court appearances, depositions, and the like. A tactic, ultimately which worked in her favor, when she later changed lawyers.

Then there was the issue of having to sell the house. By the time this was ordered by the divorce judge, a judge that seemed a little more pleasant than the criminal law judges, although Renee had warned her he was a very 'pro-male's rights kind-a-guy,' Ashley was over the whole 'dream' life thing. She felt worn out from the visits to the lawyers, and trying to avoid bumping into any of her friends at all costs for fear they may deduce something was 'up,' forcing her to muster a host of excuses. The DUI restricting her driving to certain times of day, and the children who were becoming more demanding of her time than before, the growing stress in their home, and a missing father, it was all too much. It was at this point in her life, Ashley had contact with Lily for the first time.

Their initial contact was over the phone, two weeks into the month of December. Ari needed her mother to set definite plans with David's mother so she could join them for dinner and the Christmas *Jingle Ball* show. Lily was easy to talk to, and made some off the wall joke about Woodfield to which Ashley strangely connected, and the two of them spoke for a good while discussing life in Woodfield. They felt an instant connection. It was fluid, and comfortable for Ashley.

The next time Lily saw Ashley was at Ashley's home when she went round to drop Ari off before the *Jingle Ball* show. They were casually chatting about David and Ari's

WOODFIELD, a gated community

school performance in Ashley's living room when Lily noticed the peace dove at the top of their very tall Christmas tree. She commented about how unique she thought it was to have a peace dove rather than an Angel or a star at the top of her tree, and how it blessed her home with peace from above, and how peace would surround her and her family this Christmas.

At that moment, Ashley burst into hysterical tears, splattering words between each sob, "and that is all I want peace...peace for me and my family...How could he take our peace away like that?...Poor David, he so wanted....I can't take this fighting any more!"

Now this kind of an incident, while totally foreign to someone like Ashley, was very common to someone like Lily. Lily was very familiar with having woman burst into tears out of the blue over something she had said. It was as she always understood, a message would come through from a higher source which hit the center heart beat of the other person, collapsing them instantly into a ball of tears. But tears were a form of release, surrender, an opportunity for change.

Lily placed her arms around Ashley, and tried to comfort her, letting her know everything would work out, she was merely passing through a time of events which needed to be resolved. She was shedding a part of her life which would no longer serve her in the near future. Ashley found Lily's presence very soothing, but confusing because she was not accustomed to conversing with a perfect stranger who instantly understood her so easily. It was like Lily could read her deepest thoughts.

This was Lily's innate talent. Others looking at Ashley from the outside, and hearing her day to day conversations would not believe she was even capable of deep thoughts, and so over time, Ashley had come to internalize this belief herself. But Lily knew otherwise, everyone had powerful deep inner thoughts. These were the thoughts which needed to be watered, fertilized and nurtured, for these were the latent natural talents of a Soul which existed to truly be of service to the world.

This fear that Lily was almost a perfect stranger to Ashley, didn't derail Ashley completely, Lily's presence was far too overwhelming. She had deep penetrating green eyes which seemed to lock you comfortably in her gaze encouraging you to release the flood gates of your pain. So, for the next 20 minutes Ashley filled Lily in on her life – her main focus being, Joe. How could he have done this to her? How could he be so cruel? Uncaring? Irrational? Insensitive? Ashley was at a loss.

Then Lily said, "consider this Ashley, what if you did this to him in a previous life? What if you were as cruel and mean to him as he is being to you now? What if you left him in that life to care for the children? What if you were the husband in that previous life, and he the wife?"

That image of Joe being her, made Ashley laugh, which Lily was happy about, lightened her energy, she thought.

"What are you saying Lily?" asked Ashley.

"Well, do you believe we have lived on this Planet before?"

"Oh, Absolutely," answered Ashley, "but I haven't given it much thought in years, and I would never have thought of connecting it to my life today. You see, when I was a child of four, my mother said I would ask her to take me to my aunt Betty because she was my *other* mother, and then I would go on to describe some other existence with my aunt Betty as my mother. My aunty Betty and I have always had an unusually close relationship, especially when I was younger. Eventually, my mother said I got older, and stopped talking about it. Hmmmm."

"Okay," said Lily breaking Ashley's train of thought, "let's follow through with this. If this was the case, then you Ashley are NOT a victim. So you should stop thinking about yourself as a victim. Anyway, regardless of this, you should stop seeing yourself as a victim in life. You're not a victim Ashley, you have merely made choices in your life, not mistakes, which have made your path a little turbulent. No one can control life Ashley, that's the irony of it, you just feel under-confident about yourself, and so you feel like you're sinking, that's all. You need to know the moment you stop thinking about yourself as a victim in this world, and in your life, you start to see things differently and your life begins to miraculously change."

Ashley sat and listened. Everything Lily said, seemed to sit perfectly deep down. She couldn't work it out, but it just felt right. At that point, Ashley's parents began to grow impatient. They had dinner reservations scheduled before the *Jingle Ball* so they could get the younger children home directly after the show.

"I'm really going to think about what you said Lily," said Ashley.

"Good. And you need to get back into your artwork. It's time to bring out those old canvases and start painting again, Ashley. Painting is very therapeutic especially for someone as artistic as you."

Ashley froze. She had been cleaning out a closet yesterday, and stumbled upon all her art supplies, including her easel.

"I know, it is time isn't it?" Ashley agreed in a soft voice still recovering from the shock.

"Yes, it is Ashley, and you really should welcome the change, for change is the only constant in our lives, and our greatest friend. I couldn't imagine anything worse than never meeting anyone new or situations in our lives never changing and lasting forever. I can see you really need to get going. Thanks for inviting Ari, and I hope to see you again soon." And with that she was gone.

Ashley felt a wonderful lightness that evening, one she had not felt in a long, long time. It was as if a dark cloud had miraculously lifted off her shoulders, one she didn't even realize was there.

Shortly after her meeting with Lily, Ashley changed lawyers. While it cost her a good deal more money, she hired a lawyer who was board certified in Florida family law, taking a major step in leveling the playing field with Joe. Joe's mother,

Ashley believed, had hand picked his lawyer, making absolutely sure he would get the best representation money could buy, although Joe, wanting everything 'wrapped' up already, often gave little attention to the details. All he wanted was to get back to Mel.

And get back to Mel he did, as often as he could. This separation from Ashley suited him down to the ground. He was free every other weekend, and during the week when he was permitted to have the children for the night, there was always his mother, if he was out of town. Ashley was a thing of the past. His shinning new life in New York awaited him, and that is all he occupied his mind with. He had the potential of a new job in a leading brokerage house on Wall Street, and all he focused on or wanted to focus on was making money. Yet, he followed through with whatever ploy his lawyer devised for him, anything to keep his mother from breathing down his neck. She had become quite obsessed with her revenge on Ashley, even though he knew Ashley really had played a very limited part in orchestrating the whole ordeal, and hadn't initially hired a big name lawyer for their divorce either, although he knew she certainly had the means to.

Lily was right, Ashley thought. As soon as she started surrendering her victim mentality things started to change. She stopped fighting life head on so much, and made an effort to let the day take her at will. She began to see she couldn't accomplish everything in a day, and what didn't get done that day, didn't get done. There was always the next day. There really wasn't any rush in life.

With this new force in place, she was even able to secure a night with Jennifer, the babysitter from next door. The one, her neighbors would 'shoo' away, if anyone got close to her. It happened early one evening when Ashley was fumbling around in her car looking for Madison's favorite toy, Madison screaming in the background, devastated by her loss. Jennifer drove up and parked her car in the driveway alongside Ashley's car. It was bizarre, Ashley recalled, but Jennifer got out her car, waved to Ashley, and began a conversation with her over how crazy Florida drivers were, and before Ashley knew it Jennifer was accepting a babysitting job with her children the following evening. Ashley's parents were still in town for the next couple of weeks, and the three of them were in needed of a quiet adult-only dinner.

The funny thing was however, Ashley's children didn't feel comfortable with cute, trendy Jennifer, they had grown fond of their Nina and Olivia. Ashley noticed the children seemed to be changing too. It was as Lily later told her, your children react to how you are. If you feel hysterical and unbalanced inside then that's the type of energy you give off. Children pick up on this energy and respond back to you in the same manner. There is no other way for them to react. You attract in another human, Lily tried to rationalize for Ashley, what you energize, or give off. It was this simple. And so it was. Jennifer seemed to be an attraction to an older energy, an energy which had shifted, and no longer thrived in Ashley's life. She never asked Jennifer to babysit again.

The next day, again something magical happened. Marge called and told her all the criminal charges against her for the DUI had been dropped, and the State was prepared to lower the Reckless driving charge to a traffic infraction. Marge was sure she could send the traffic infraction to a lawyer friend of hers who handled traffic charges. Something about lack of evidence, conflicting testimonies from the officers in deposition, and no video tape of the DUI investigation. Marge also said she had handled a full investigative hearing at the DMV the day before, and was waiting for a decision from them. She told Ashley to keep her fingers crossed because she felt she may have a good shot at winning that hearing also.

The light was beginning to shine over Ashley.

Chapter SEVEN

In any law suit, one of the most challenging times is during the discovery phase. Throughout discovery both sides are working at gathering information to make their points of view stronger. In family law cases, this can be particularly emotionally demanding on the parties, mostly because this stage may involve several court hearings, demands on both sides to produce a massive collection of documents, and depositions. All the emotions we teach our children over the years to keep under wraps, and never to reveal under any circumstances, sit in wait for these times.

During any one court hearing a lawyer can encounter with a client an assortment of emotions which run the gamut between anger, shock, denial, hatred, impatience, revenge, distrust, blinded fury, and destruction. Any possible chance of rational thought from a client in a divorce case is often seriously remote. Any lawyer worth their salt is as emotionally detached from the case, and the players as possible.

Another important aspect to being a good family lawyer is being able to evaluate a potential client upon meeting them for the first time. It is necessary to determine whether this person will be a good performer when they take the stand, one who needs polishing, or one who will need a substantial amount of skill refining. Ashley, according to Andy Gold, fell somewhere between good, and needing polishing. Mostly because, he decided, she had already been exposed to some aspect of the divorce courts, in that, she was looking to switch lawyers. He preferred these kinds of clients rather than those fresh in the game because they usually would arrive with a stronger attitude knowing exactly what they didn't want. When clients know what they don't want, it is far easier to determine where the jumping off point in a case should be. It allows you to move into the fray, with fresh initiative, generating a force which will move it forward more rapidly, which is commonly the aim of the majority of spouses getting divorced.

This speed would also generate a substantial amount of billable hours which Andy Gold referred to as positive reinforcement for himself, as he would navigate through every possible trick in the book. Anyone, hiring him knew he was going to cost, and cost Andy Gold did, billing at a tender fifteen hundred per hour for his expertise, and a six figure retainer. All initial consultations ran at two thousand per hour, and Andy was very particular about which cases he would take. Those cases usually entailed ones which wouldn't run out of money. His main concern, he would tell potential clients, is that he never wanted his hands tied in a case. If the other side moved their knight, he wanted to be able to move his queen, and fast. And, to achieve this he always needed a strong retainer in his trust account. He never asked his clients to replenish a retainer account with him, he just anticipated they would automatically do so, as soon as it was depleted to half.

Andy Gold was also top on the list of the divorce shoppers. Divorce shoppers were those spouses who would go around having as many consultations with divorce lawyers as possible, creating a block for their spouse ever being able to hire that lawyer. In Florida no-one could hire a lawyer after they had been consulted by their spouse, it would create a huge conflict of interest because of the very strong attorney-client privilege. Mary Weeks, was in charge of being diligently sure Andy did not consult with a potential conflict. Andy always had a sizeable amount of shoppers each month, he could pick them out immediately, but he loved them all just as much. They refilled his coffers monthly, and he got to meet and greet a variety of people, often developing useful contacts for his private loves, such as art collecting, fine dining, and travel.

And true to his word, Andy Gold produced a landslide of paperwork for the other side, which he began the moment Ashley left his office. Every day for two weeks his secretary Mary Weeks, would be furiously typing up demands, motions, amendments, and any other type of document Andy Gold could conjure up which would inundate the other side, and the Clerk of Court. He would then hire an array of professionals on the sidelines, like private investigators, forensic accountants, additional temporary office staff, and strong proof readers to review each legal document Mary had typed up before it left his office. Ashley loved it. Andy Gold was her knight in shining armor.

He called her constantly, asking her questions and confirming each detail before sending out any paperwork. He would deliver the documents by messenger, and by certified registered return receipt mail, first sending everything via facsimile and e-mail, just in case the messenger died en route to delivering the documents, or the post office went on strike. Andy Gold was big on back up. This meant for Ashley, a massive home file labeled: Copies of all Divorce proceedings, and for Andy Gold a relaxing vacation in the Swiss Alps following the case.

Andy Gold knew all the judges in the family law courts in all three surrounding counties, many of them on a first name basis. He would meet them for lunches and out on the golf course. He was slick, serious, and good at what he did, and so felt justified in being paid handsomely for it. His secretary, Mary Weeks, had been with him for twenty years, and to keep clients abreast of their retainer accounts she kept a rigid accounting of all his billable hours for each client. He was in this day and age a man to be reckoned with in the court room. Exactly what Ashley was looking for.

But no matter how good the lawyer, and how well the preparation beforehand, the client alone sits in the deposition chair being deposed by the other side. Depositions encompass a laundry list of questions prepared by the opposing side designed to exploit every possible angle of your life, past, present, and future. They can continue for hours, sometimes days, and are designed to frustrate, annoy, aggravate, and drip by drip break down the deposed. They can take several weeks to schedule because they have to be set up at a time convenient to the lawyers and their clients, or client's witnesses. Most of Andy Gold's clients had busy lives, but if he felt a certain day and time was essential for your case, as he anticipated his future court petitions, then come hell or high waters, that deposition would be set on their calendars on that particular day.

While it is customary to have a court reporter present, many depositions today are also video taped. Andy Gold didn't mind this, because it gave clients an opportunity to review their performance after depositions, to determine where they performed superbly and where they needed improvement. However, to often annoy opposing counsel and for strategic reasons Andy Gold would devise a series of court hearings vehemently opposing the depositions being video taped, never letting on to the fact, it was really his hope to actually loose this part of the case. It was essential to his overall plan. His performance upholding his argument not to permit the video taping of his client during a deposition was always highly believable and flawless.

He would pace the courtroom using all its available square footage, waving his arms in animation, pulling out his cloth hankie to wipe his brow, pausing where necessary, sitting down often in a nearby chair to regain his composure, and quoting line upon line of legal drivel from recent Supreme Court opinions across the country. All the while his legal intern furiously scribbling down notes trying to keep up. Andy Gold always required his interns to ask questions after every hearing, it was an essential aspect to learning for him, and he demanded it religiously from all his interns.

By loosing a hearing like this one in a case, one which Andy didn't care much about, was very important to him. He always had to lose at least one or two hearings per case, mainly because he didn't want to look like he was strong arming the judge. Especially, when it was his plan to swoop in during the final hearing, and win the majority of his demands for his client, if not all of them. Taking home the prize, the final prize his clients wanted, whether this was what he had suggested or not, was his only aim. His aim for Ashley was to convince the court she was the most logical choice as primary parent for the children over Joe.

The result of his clients having to be deposed before a camera fashioned one more important incentive for Andy Gold. He always invested in a good local actor. Andy Gold himself had been an aspiring actor in college, once. He double majored in Drama and Criminal Justice at Columbia in New York City. He had developed a list of actors over the years he determined good, very good and excellent. Clients needed to know how to dress, sit, look alert, when to pause, how to express a memory slip, when to burst into uncontrollable tears, and when to develop an allergy attack. And for all this, strong acting lessons for several weeks beforehand were essential.

Having dealt with a number of Ashleys over the years Andy Gold felt confident he could transform little *Ms. Shopaholic* into the perfect caring overwrought mother. One who could stand up in any prime time television program and mobilize hundreds to sympathize with her predicament of having had to destroy her life, and the lives of her children as result of her husband's philandering.

She had the captivating beauty, and in Ashley's case, he felt the intelligence, although rather hidden beneath layers of dirt accumulated from spending far too much time deciding on colors, styles, and designs for her personal wardrobe, and decorating her home.

Ashley thrived in her drama classes Andy Gold had set up for her. She would go home afterwards, and during any moment when she passed a mirror she would practice, practice,

practice. If there was one thing Ashley planned to do, it was to get to a place where her performance was faultless. During the final week of classes Ashley had to bring in an array of suits and dresses from her closet. Together she and her Drama teacher chose her deposition wardrobe. They chose three outfits which were a definite, and three backups. They anticipated her deposition taking several days.

Although, the focus was on Ashley and her deposition, she had no idea how extremely important, and compelling the depositions of Joe, and Joe's mother would turn out to be. After all, this was another opportunity for Andy Gold to shine, and shine he did.

Andy Gold always arrived a good forty minutes early to every deposition he was taking. He wanted to be sure he set up the deposition room exactly right. He liked to position himself, the court reporter, and the witness in a particular place ensuring opposing counsel would be seated in an awkward angle to their witness. This way he could minimize all body language and cues he or she may send in the direction of their witnesses which would guide them as to what to say when the questions got trickier.

Andy was immaculately dressed in a navy pin stripped suit, a personally tailored white shirt and bowtie, and an exquisitely styled handmade pair of shoes crafted in the mountains of Italy.

"I spend so much time on my feet," he would say, "that I have to wear only the most comfortable shoes!"

Hence an over abundance of exceedingly 'posh' shoes could be found housed in his closet. He also always liked to wear a white orchid during depositions and court hearings -- something about the beauty of the flower keeping his senses alert.

He was always accompanied by Mary Weeks, his legal intern, and his client. Andy brought his client along because he liked to make the witness feel uneasy by their presence. However, doing so also placed him in a precarious situation because clients, as he knew only too well, were emotional and could potentially blow up at the slightest provocation from a statement made by the witness. So, he would have to threaten his clients in a big way before they arrived, in an effort to elicit only the finest behavior from them.

"If you do not listen to me, and keep yourself composed as we have shown you these past few months, then I will stop the deposition right there and then, and petition the court to dismiss me from the case because we have irreconcilable differences. Not only will you lose a good lawyer, but you will weaken your case, making it extremely difficult for any lawyer to step into my shoes. So, please let us be on the same page here."

Marjorie Patterson, Joe's mother was first up. Marjorie, Ashley had described to Andy was a raving snob who hated Ashley's guts. She held the belief Ashley was beneath her husband's social standing and intelligence, and therefore the less able parent of the two to be left to raise the children. After all, Ashley had made such a mess of her first marriage, and then there was her son David from the first marriage.

~ 113 ~

After the court reporter had Marjorie take the oath to tell the truth, and nothing but the truth, Andy Gold began. The video lights focused on Marjorie were very bright almost blinding. This always helped to create a good haze between the witness and his clients, especially when the witnesses would get rattled by his line of questioning. Bright lights tend to daze those not accustomed to it, unlike actors of course. But Ashley was ready for the bright lights. All her acting lessons had been performed under bright lights.

"Ma'am, can you please state your name for the record."

"Yes. Mrs. Marjorie Patterson." Marjorie sat straight like a rod in her chair, chest out, one leg neatly positioned over the other, her hair immaculately styled. She wore a white Channel suit with a pale pink blouse, and a pair of dainty crimson Italian sandals. Her fragrance was so intense Ashley could smell it from where she was sitting. Michael Kors, Ashley thought. I gave it to her on her last birthday. Ashley remembered Marjorie turning her nose up to the gift, by asking where she had bought it, should she decide to exchange it. Obviously, she never did.

"Mrs. Patterson, thank you for coming today," Andy said politely, although, everyone knew once subpoenaed for deposition, short of a court ruling canceling it, you had no choice but to show up.

"Do you know the Respondent in this case, Mrs. Ashley Loveit?" Andy continued.

"Yes," Marjorie answered curtly without even looking in Ashley's direction.

"Can you state your relationship to her?"

Marjorie coughed, "She's my daughter-in-law, or was…."

Cutting her short, Andy asked, "and how would you describe your relationship with your daughter in law, Mrs. Patterson?"

"Rocky," said Marjorie.

"I see you rolling your eyes Mrs. Patterson. Why? Don't you like her?"

Delighted Andy picked up on her intended insult towards Ashley, Marjorie continued more animated, "Well, for one thing she has no clue what so ever how to raise kids!" Andy let her continue.

"She is always off with her friends and leaving them with those incompetent nannies. She has no idea when to stop feeding them sugar, dresses them like clowns, has no set time for them to go to bed, and the children keep crying at the slightest of things."

"So, you just don't like Mrs. Loveit because she is an irresponsible mother, is that what you trying to tell me here Mrs. Patterson?"

"Absolutely right," responded Marjorie loudly thinking she had said it all, and made Ashley's case burn up in her face. She thought once the judge hears *that*, it will all be over for poor Ashley.

"Do you believe Mrs. Patterson that 'you' know the correct way to raise children?"

"Oh, yes I do. I certainly do, and it isn't in any way like she does," Marjorie said elated believing she had made a valid point, and finally found a sympathetic ear.

"Do you believe you have always known how to raise children Mrs. Patterson?"

"Oh, yes, it is just natural to me. Inborn. Some just have it," said Marjorie unable to confine herself to answering yes or no. And, Andy was just warming her up.

"Tell, me Mrs. Patterson just how do you think you should raise children, I mean what kind of rules should you have?" Andy asked.

"Well, you should always be there as a mother, no matter what. Friends take a back seat, just like earning money. You give it all up. You stay home, you cook and feed your kids the correct balanced meals, you do it no matter what. You have set times for them to go to bed, you never leave them alone with sitters for hours on end," Marjorie answered.

"Is that everything then Mrs. Patterson to ensure a well raised child?"

"Mostly, what I can think of off hand," Marjorie answered haughtily.

"Is this how *you* raised Joe, Mrs. Patterson, the way you describe it?" Andy turned to the court reporter and asked her to read back Marjorie's testimony beginning with the words "you should always be there as a mother..."

"Yes. Exactly how I raised my boy," she confirmed with her usual "know-it-all" attitude.

"And do you think, based on this, your son should be the primary parent for his children?" Andy asked.

"Yes. I do. He knows how I raised him, and he will, in turn, know how to raise his children," she said, once again volunteering more than asked of her.

Joe's lawyer began to shift in his chair. He knew Andy Gold had something up his sleeve. He knew him all too well. Steve Silver had come up against Andy several times over the years. He respected him greatly as a lawyer, and knew he always had a plan. Not that Steve himself was too shabby a lawyer, but he knew when Andy was around, he needed to step up his game plan. He also knew stepping in at every turn in a deposition to object was futile especially when it came to Andy, it only caused delays, and more paperwork, and the case law was fairly lenient in what could and could not be derived from depositions, so he let Andy proceed unfettered.

"Mrs Patterson, were you raised by both your parents?"

"Yes."

"Where did you live growing up?"

"Chicago."

"Did you move a lot as a child?"

"Yes."

"Why?"

"My father kept changing jobs," Marjorie shifted in her chair, and became visibly uncomfortable. She didn't seem to be enjoying this line of questioning. Ashley, on the other hand, of course, was becoming very interested in it.

"And why was that Mrs. Patterson?"

"He kept loosing his job."

"Why did he keep loosing his job Mrs. Patterson?"

And in a much softer tone than before, Marjorie responded, "He drank a lot."

"How old were you when your father passed?"

"Thirteen," Marjorie answered. All her answers had become very, very short.

"How did he die?"

"From alcohol poisoning," she said shifting in her chair.

"Objection!" said Steve Silver, "this is about the grandchildren not their great grandfather!"

"Yes, I do get that point, counselor, however, if you would just indulge me, I will get to my point," Steve asked the Court reporter to make the objection on file, and certify it for a court hearing.

"And, Mrs. Patterson, how did your mother die?

"From an overdose," Marjorie said, using the same low pitch she used when answering questions about her father.

Ashley was stunned. She had no idea Marjorie had such a harsh upbringing. She felt a little sorry for her sitting up there. Then, she remembered this woman wanted to take her children to live with her and Joe for most of the time, a thought which sobered Ashley quickly.

"How old were you Mrs. Patterson when your mother died?"

"Seventeen."

"Were you still living at home with your mother?"

"Yes."

"What did you do after your mother died?"

"I kept the house going, dropped out of school and got a job," Marjorie responded, looking down at her hands which now lay intertwined in her lap.

"Was that address…" Andy shuffled his papers looking for something.

Ashley saw the report as it emerged from a pile. Mary Weeks had neatly added an index number, and attached it to the top right hand corner, no doubt so Andy could easily retrieve it when he needed.

"1422 West Martin Street," Andy read out loudly.

Marjorie looked up suddenly in shock. "Yes," was her short but clear response. Ashley was beginning to feel Andy Gold was dangerously close to something. Andy was unmoved.

"Now where exactly was it that you worked?" Andy asked, shuffling more papers, which seemed to now cause Steve Silver to shift in his seat in trepidation.

"I don't remember, it was a long time ago," answered Marjorie. Ashley began to notice the very composed Marjorie, the one who walked into her deposition, nose held high, was rapidly beginning to dissolve.

"You sure you don't remember Mrs. Patterson?"

"Yes."

"Perhaps if I give you a copy of a paystub you received back then it may help jog your memory, Mrs. Patterson?" Andy passed Steve a photocopy of the pay stub, and one to the court reporter. Addressing the court reporter, he asked that it be entered as 'Exhibit One.'

"Please look at the copy of this pay stub Mrs. Patterson, and tell me if you remember receiving these paystubs?"

When Marjorie received the piece of paper Ashley saw all the color in Marjorie's face drain, and her shoulders hunch over. There was no denying it, Marjorie Patterson wanted to be anywhere else on Earth, but where she was right now.

"Yes," she answered in a very low voice.

"And for what work was this Mrs. Patterson?"

"A topless bar," answered Marjorie ever so quietly.

Ashley's jaw dropped. This bitch! This bitch, who always professed to be the high and mighty! Who would have ever known?

"And, Mrs. Patterson, tell me were you still working here when your son Joe was born?" Andy said, not stopping.

"Yes," Marjorie replied very quietly.

"And when you were out working Mrs. Patterson who looked after Joe?"

"My neighbor Annie, and sometimes Ettie my other neighbor."

"And, how old was Annie Mrs. Patterson, when she was looking after Joe?"

"Sixteen."

"And how many children did Ettie have of her own, around the time Joe was born?"

"Five."

"Ettie had five children, other than Joe to look after?"

"Yes. I said five didn't I?" Marjorie said, desperately trying to regain her high and mighty composure, by showing disdain for this endless line of questioning.

"And did you leave food out for Joe to eat?"

"I really have no idea where this is all going," said Marjorie, squinting her eyes, desperately searching for Steve Silver through the bright light. The lawyer *she* hired for *her* son. But Steve sat silent looking down at his legal note pad.

"Please just answer the question Mrs. Patterson," Andy re-instructed firmly.

"Yes. The answer to your question is *yes*," she said using a higher and firmer pitch for the word 'yes.'

"What kind of food Mrs. Patterson?"

"Whatever I could pick up in-between my jobs."

"Oh, so you had two jobs?"

"Yesssss," Marjorie answered in a condescending tone.

"What was your other job?" Andy continued, unaffected.

"I was an assistant hair stylist, in a neighborhood salon called *Uncut*," Marjorie answered, turning her body towards the wall on her left, and crossing her one arm over her midriff joining it to the other.

"Over the next several years you worked in many different strip clubs in Chicago; Kingsbury Street, Ontario Street, and Freemont Street, isn't that right Mrs. Patterson?"

"Yes." Marjorie had stopped volunteering any extra information.

Ashley was beginning to see why Joe was so hung up on making money, and lots of it. Money was Joe's driving force.

"Did you date, Mrs. Patterson, when Joe was a young child?" asked Andy moving onto another subject.

"Yes."

"When you went out on dates did you leave Joe with Annie or Ettie?"

"No, mostly with Maxie," she said slowly.

"How old was Maxie?" Andy continued to press the point.

"I don't remember. She worked at *Uncut*."

"How old was Joe when you met Mr. Patterson?" he asked casually.

Marjorie outwardly relaxed again, thinking the pressure had lessoned with a change in topic, "Three."

"Was this the only father figure Joe ever had?" Andy asked casually.

"Yes," Marjorie responded.

"Has Joe ever met his biological father?" Andy pushed on.

"Objection!" Steve Silver jumped up out of his seat, "what in heaven's name has that got to do with anything?" Steve questioned Andy with a raised voice. Inside Andy was smiling, and Steve knew it. Steve wouldn't be Steve if he didn't jump up at least once during a deposition. After all, Steve was well versed in theatrics too.

"Everything counselor," Andy responded calmly in contrast to Steve's hysteria, "we are discussing Mrs. Patterson's child rearing skills, are we not?"

"Exactly, " responded Steve, "not biological fathers. That is purely irrelevant, and I will move to strike this from the record, and motion to have it excluded in trial," Steve said firmly.

"I tell you what counselor," Andy said, "I will respect your objection, and we can bring a hearing before the judge about this issue, and if I win the hearing, I reserve the right here and now to bring Mrs. Patterson back to follow this line of questioning. Agreed?"

Marjorie didn't like the sound of this at all, and speaking out loud said, "I really want this over with now, I don't want to come back." The two men looked at one another. These were the kind of moments Andy loved in depositions.

"Well, I'm sorry Mrs. Patterson, but opposing counsel has made himself quite clear, and I am not in a position to override him," Andy said skillfully. So, let's continue shall we.

"How long were you married for Mrs. Patterson, to Mr. Patterson I mean?"

"Five long years. What a waste of a man *he* was…" she said, as if *she* had no part in the failed marriage.

"No doubt he didn't meet your high standards either, Mrs. Patterson?" Andy played.

"No. Promised the world, but never delivered on anything," she shared rolling her eyes and shifting in her seat.

"Tell me, Mrs. Patterson, during your marriage to Mr. Patterson, did you change your employment or remain at the clubs and *Uncut*?" Andy waited patiently for this point.

"Changed to another club, because he didn't like the one I was at, and got promoted to stylist, for whatever that was worth! Never made much more money," she said, now lost as to Andy's game plan.

"You divorced Mr. Patterson?" Andy asked casually.

"You bet! He ran off with a woman from the club. He was having…"

Andy stopped her, "That is fine, thank you, Mrs. Patterson."

Then Andy summed up. "So, let me get this straight Mrs. Patterson. You worked in several topless bars, and *Uncut*. You were seldom home. You left your son to be taken care of by one babysitter that was sixteen years old, and another who already had five other children of her own. You didn't cook for your son, and you played no part in putting your son to bed at a regular time? Is this all correct?"

Marjorie didn't answer. She knew she had been horribly trapped. But Andy persisted, coming at the jugular, "Please answer my question Mrs. Patterson."

"Yes," she said quietly.

"And then when you dated men, which you claim you did, you left your son with Maxie, whose age or other details you don't recall. This, totaling, let me see, *three* different babysitters, taking care of your son at one time?"

"Yes, I already told you," she said growing more agitated.

"But then, even after you married Mr. Patterson, you didn't change this pattern either. Is that correct?" Andy said raising his pitch a notch.

"Yes, I told you," Marjorie answered now exasperated by this annoying man. Had he not been listening to a word she said.

"Now, didn't you say earlier, Mrs. Patterson, and I quote back your very own words: *Well, you should always be there as a mother, no matter what. Friends take a back seat, just like earning money. You give it all up. You stay home, you cook and feed your kids the correct balanced meals, you do it no matter what. You have set times for them to go to bed, you never leave them alone with sitters for hours on end?'* Andy asked.

No response from Marjorie.

"Well, Mrs. Patterson, didn't you say this an hour ago?" Please make note on the record that I am being forced to make the witness answer the question.

"Yes," said Marjorie confused.

"And, Mrs. Patterson, didn't you also say an hour ago that this was how you raised your son? If I recall your words went something like this, 'Yes. *Exactly* how I raised my boy!' Andy said exaggerating the word 'exactly.'

"Yes," said Marjorie again beginning to get the point.

"But that is not true is it Mrs. Patterson, you didn't raise your boy the way you said you did earlier, did you?"

"No," said Marjorie. Marjorie's face was now shining brightly under the video lights as beads of sweat formed around

~ 127 ~

her brow, and began to trickle down the side of her hairline. The calm, cool, and collected Marjorie was no more. But nothing stopped Andy Gold.

"And, yet you clearly have standards for Mrs. Loveit, don't you, Mrs. Patterson?" Andy asked and stated simultaneously.

"Yes, I mean they are my grandchildren," Marjorie said fumbling for some thread of dignity.

"But, Joe is your son, is he not?" Andy persisted shredding her dignity once more.

"Yes," Marjorie said cautiously.

"No less important than your grandchildren, right Mrs. Patterson?"

"Yes," Marjorie said completely trapped.

"Isn't that all a little bit hypocritical Mrs. Patterson?" Andy kept pushing.

"Objection," said Steve Silver, "badgering the witness. You made your point."

"Mrs. Patterson in light of your circumstances, and how you raised your own son, don't you think your grandchildren are not too badly off being raised by Mrs. Loveit in Woodfield Suburban Club?" Andy asked, ready to pounce if she ever thought of saying 'no' to this one.

Marjorie was silent.

"Mrs. Patterson my question requires a response," pressed Andy, and he repeated the question.

"I guess," was all Marjorie could bring herself to say.

"I assume you mean 'yes,' Mrs. Patterson," flaunted Andy.

"Yes."

"Mrs. Patterson," Andy continued, "isn't it true that Joe travels a great deal?"

"Yes."

"And when he travels you take care of the children?"

"Yes."

"Do you own your own home Mrs. Patterson?

"Yes."

"Did you buy it for yourself?"

"No," Marjorie's tone was softer again. Ashley became more focused. She was familiar now with Andy's tactics.

"Who bought your home for you then Mrs. Patterson?"

"My son, Joe," she answered.

Ashley's mouth dropped open. She had no idea Joe bought and paid for Marjorie's home out of joint marital funds.

"Do you know if your son plans on staying in Florida?"

"I don't know, you will have to ask him that yourself," Marjorie responded curtly.

"Thank you Mrs. Patterson I will do that," Andy answered humoring her.

Marjorie's deposition went on for hours. Every aspect of Marjorie's life was exposed in an attempt to determine what would ultimately be in the best interest of Ashley and Joe's children.

At the end, Steve Silver took over questioning Marjorie, in re-direct, trying to clean up some of the mess she had created in her son's case. He wasn't too successful, but that wasn't because he was a bad lawyer or lacked experience, he was an excellent lawyer, and the very reason why Ashley had to find herself an Andy Gold. But, Andy Gold's private investigator was one of the best, and had clearly come through for him today by unearthing many personal documents relating to Marjorie's life back in Chicago.

Ashley felt rather satisfied after Marjorie's deposition, but Andy warned her not to get too comfortable as they still had a way to go. Joe's deposition was up next in a few weeks, and while Ashley felt confident with Andy, at the same time she secretly didn't enjoy being at odds with Joe like this, however, she never let on to Andy about her feelings. She didn't have to, Andy already knew, Ashley was no exception to the rule.

Chapter EIGHT

Once in a while a particular female will comb the Florida Suburban club social scene. She is usually of a distinct type. She sees what she wants, sends out subliminal messages enticing her prey, and then creates a medley of impediments between herself and her quarry, generating an escalating desire and fervor in the various cortex centers of the male brain.

This woman, is the Woodfield women's deadliest opponent, she is skillful and her sexual prowess unparalleled. But, unlike the Woodfield women, as soon as she has absorbed all she can from her male prize, paralyzing him with her penetrating, unrelenting demands, turning their lives inside out and upside down (which they seem to relish, and so continue to linger around in a trance for more), she discards them, rendering them useless.

Amelia Swift, was one of those woman who proudly and justifiably so, wore the title of *The Black Widow*. And, like all Black Widows, Amelia didn't believe in the concept of love. She was a purebred career woman, in an overpopulated man's world. To Amelia, Bella, the female star in *Beauty and the Beast* was set and headed for a promising career but developed a weakness, a love of animals, and so derailed her life, tumbling into the depths of frivolity.

Anyone remotely versed in Astrology, would know upon meeting Amelia that she had the perfect Black Widow profile. She had a Scorpio sun sign providing her with the mysterious, magnetic, and hypnotic talents which intoxicated so many men in her world. She disliked being possessed by anyone, had a love for power, and very conscious of the social standing she had achieved in her life, and she would never compromise in the case of status. She had a storehouse of secrets, but no one knew any of hers. She was determined, and owned a strong willpower. Once Amelia chose her target she could become extremely fierce in taking possession.

Two other aspects in Amelia's astrological chart allowed her to remain aloof and detached when it came to the men in her life. Most of the time she took them by surprise, because, it lay in such sharp contrast to the Scorpio energy she would portray. Her emotions were dominated by an Aquarian Moon sign, and Aquarius occupied Venus in her profile when it came to love matters. This accounted for a very non-traditional outlook on relationships. She was the rebel in love.

This could be an attraction for many men who preferred the more progressive, open radical minded partner who refused to obey traditional rules of love. But for the traditional male looking for love, Amelia proved to be a massive, if not impossible goal to attain. Keeping her further out of reach was her discomfort with self pity or anyone self absorbed in their emotions. She did, however, find herself in emotional turmoil if her trust was broken, or her dreams crushed, but this was seldom the case.

Her counterbalance, to being the champion of the status quo, and a successful snob, through all of this detachment, and uninvolved emotion, was she could just as easily take the side of the underdog. She had a hidden passion for humanity, and found great comfort in helping one worse off. Everything depended on how she was feeling at the time.

Her Leo rising sign was often the dominant side in her life, and the one most people would be confronted with upon first meeting Amelia. Through the force in this sign she would desire to be a shinning star, and stand out as an individual. She instinctively radiated an energy that got her noticed. Her regal manner always seemed to be a draw, and as a result she dedicated a great deal of attention to her personal appearance, especially her hair.

She made very sure her appearance matched the backdrop to her life – The backdrop comprising of the people she was around and the environment she played in. She was an excellent promoter, and possessed an inherent flare for presentation, partly because drama came so naturally to her. She had a strong desire to oversee the goings on in her circles, which could sometimes amount to bossiness unless kept in check.

Her Leo rising sign did have the tendency to make her appear to others as prone to rash decisions, temper tantrums, and excesses. From time to time she would over estimate things, and herself, but that was often due to her intrinsic enthusiasm and optimism about any new undertaking. Strangely, in her own life, she could sometimes be caught up in the fiction, and be a little blind to fact. To offset this aspect of her chart: Other people's talents and success inspired her. She applauded and appreciated individuality, creativity, the spirit, and joy of life wherever she saw it being expressed. Warmth and benevolence on occasion could flow forth from her.

Amelia was from a lower middle class, downtown Detroit neighborhood, and had always lived a life of warding off men. These men sometimes included certain close family members. One in particular, was the cause of her leaving home as young, and as soon as she could. At that point she made a vow, to always stay aloof to the male species, and to never let her guard down. The other vow she made to herself was to be the best at what she did, whatever that turned out to be, and never be threatened by another male in her life again.

She worked her way through college, and then entered the world of marketing. Amelia became hugely successful. She owned several thriving drop shipping internet businesses, and distributed goods throughout the world. When others were investing in 401K plans, Amelia was channeling her funds into small companies, overhauling their internal systems, and subsequently selling them off at a handsome profit. Much of Amelia's livelihood also required her to do a great deal of traveling, all of which she loved. By the time she was in her mid thirties she was worth several million dollars, and in need of nothing, and dependant on no one.

But there was something Amelia did which was hidden from the outside world. A place she would go where she never invited anyone to join her, especially men. Every year she would take herself off to a remote village run by a Buddhist monastery in Sri Lanka where she spent six to eight weeks, sometimes more, doing manual labor and assisting the very poor.

When living in the village, Amelia would make two trips into town to check her e-mails on a very outdated computer which took several minutes to boot up. Nevertheless, she would tell everyone who needed to know, which was usually only her personal assistant Elizabeth, who would lip sync Amelia's words with her back to Amelia, she knew them so well.

"The world existed before me, it will no doubt exist just as easily without me." Still lip syncing, "Anything Earth shattering give to my lawyer. The lawyers are masters at delaying action. Tell them to delay it, until my return. And under no circumstances whatsoever Elizabeth, let anyone know where I am."

The last part was not too hard for Elizabeth because she really didn't know where Amelia was, this was the one location Amelia never revealed. Elizabeth had been employed by Amelia for almost a decade, and seemed to be the only female capable of understanding her, but then again she also had a very thorough understanding of astrology, and so nothing Amelia did ever surprised Elizabeth.

And so, for several weeks Amelia would pick and sort coconuts, help to harvest cinnamon spice by scrapping the outer bark of the cinnamon tree branches and prising out the thin inner bark, collecting water from streams, teaching children English, and living on a purely plant-based diet. This village was her private retreat where she could become in touch with her Soul and allow herself the opportunity to let her heart rule. It was managed by a group of Buddhist monks, and was the only place in the entire world Amelia felt completely safe and un-judged.

At the end of her stay she would pass through the nearby town one more time to order and send supplies to the monastery. The villagers and monks lived exclusively off the land and loved their subsistence. She would never send them anything which was outside their comfort zone of existence, so, her list was limited to seeds from vegetables and fruits, flour, pitchers to hold large quantities of water and food, string, hooks, blank tablets for the children to write in, pencils, erasers, and other useful items the monks wouldn't object to.

Amelia led an exciting life every day, but everything in her usual daily schedule, other than when she was in the village in Sri Lanka, was self serving. She was beginning to feel she needed to refocus, she needed something more. As she moved into her late thirties this need would be particularly prominent when she returned from the Sri Lankan village. Amelia had the propensity to develop some kind of extremism in thought. She decided she wanted to have someone or something to come home to, but that someone was definitely not going to be a man or an animal.

So, she set her plan into action. Joe Loveit, became the chosen target, the sperm donor Amelia was looking for. Why she chose Joe Loveit she wasn't quite sure. There was nothing unique about Joe, she felt. To her, he was the typically beautiful, well-sculptured male species. Bronzed, strong, handsome, and he had the right shade of blue eyes she was looking for. It may have been the particular shade of blue eyes that placed Joe in the winning seat. Whatever the case, Joe became Amelia's objective, and so she pressed, maneuvered, and rescheduled everything to bring about their encounters.

Joe contacted *The Little Apple,* company one day in search of data to research for his clients. It had recently been placed on the New York Stock Exchange as a highly sought after stock in an emerging and expanding business. Organically grown and harvested apples, peaches and pears, were globally fast becoming high in demand. When Joe called and identified himself, and his mission, he was immediately patched through to Amelia's cell phone. Amelia in turn set up a meeting with Joe and another half dozen traders, all interested in buying stock in *The Little Apple,* company. She was a master at marketing her companies, and trusted this vital task to no one else. Joe, of course, completely infatuated without even meeting this woman, agreed readily. And so the date was set.

Amelia Swift was a potent force. In any meeting she was able to play, prod, and influence every mind around the table. She made it her mission to know everyone's first and last names by the end of the meeting, regardless of the number in attendance. She had a perfectly fluid thinking brain, and details were her strong suit. Her intuition was so sharp she was sure the man in the powder blue stripped Hugo Boss open neck shirt, and dark beige pants walking towards her would introduce himself, as Joe Loveit. As soon as the dark handsome man was within range he introduced himself.

"Nice to meet you, I'm Joe Loveit," Joe said extending his hand to shake hers.

Amelia responded with her infamous smile, "very nice to meet you Joe, I'm Amelia Swift, but please, feel free to call me Amelia."

Joe, proved to be a quick, easy and playful distraction for her. He marveled at the beauty and perfection of her long legs, her purely feminine energy which Amelia so skillfully revealed to Joe, her enormous wealth, along with which came the privilege of power and being known around town, and her total freedom of movement. Amelia would fly in unannounced on any one particular night, and demand to see Joe. What Joe didn't know was she arranged their meetings based on her biology, and Joe would rush over under the pretense he had an unexpected trade to make in New York. When in reality, he would stow away to the penthouse suite Amelia always stayed in, the five star Palm Gardens Hotel overlooking the ocean, a mere twenty miles from his home.

There they would exchange bodily fluids several times, dine on oysters, mussels and lobster salad at around midnight in the suite, and when Joe would awaken in the morning, Amelia would be gone, no message left behind. The promise of nothing. Amelia got what she wanted, but Joe loved it, and he wanted Amelia, he wanted her so badly. The more elusive she made herself, the more he wanted her. He would call her on her cell phone to see where she was, and if he could get on a plane and visit her, even for one night he would. But Amelia was the proverbial executive, constantly in and out of meetings, and so Joe learned he had to wait for Amelia. When Amelia's schedule said it was Joe Loveit's play time, Joe would get his summons, and this came mostly through Elizabeth.

Amelia's interlude with Joe lasted about six months. Enough time for one of her eggs to become fertilized, and for the first trimester of high risk miscarrying to pass. She was very fertile and always knew this about herself. Those six months for Joe seemed like two. Mainly, because he would spend almost, every waking moment, thinking about Amelia, conjuring up visions of the life he was planning for the two of them. There was only one minor detail unbeknown to Joe, Amelia's dreams didn't include him, in fact, he wasn't even in the background picture for her, certainly at that point in time anyway.

Like so many species of Black Widow spiders, as soon as the mating for procreation is over the female rids herself of the male. When Amelia broke the news to Joe she thought it best they stop seeing one another, especially since he was married and about to become a father for the second time, Joe was devastated. Ashley was in her final stages of pregnancy with Madison.

"I'll leave Ashley. I don't love her. I only married her because all the guys I knew thought she was hot, and they all wanted her. I could come and live with you, and travel wherever you go. I only need a laptop to do my work. We could do business deals together. Shit Amelia, we could make a fortune together!" Joe pleaded.

They were in a hotel penthouse suite in Manhattan, New York City. Amelia poured herself a drink, sometimes a little alcohol helped her get through the well known begging stages of the male species, she often had to endure every time she parted company with them. A little alcohol here and there won't necessarily harm the baby, she had read. But it was something about the desperate plea to stay which was actually the point of no return for Amelia.

"It's over Joe. It's time for you to return to your own life. I don't love you, I never have. Now please I have a meeting first thing in the morning, I need you to leave."

"But please, Amelia," Joe whined as he tried to place his arms around her waist.

Amelia stepped back, but Joe persisted, "baby, we are so good together. Why not just give it a try. Just one try, a few weeks, come on."

Amelia was surprised, and exactly how did Joe think he was going to give it a few weeks try, she thought, even if she had asked for it? His wife was about to give birth. What kind of a lying cheating man would this be? She had to be sure she taught this child in her belly otherwise, whatever its sex.

"What part don't you understand Joe of the 'I *don't* love you, and *want* you to leave *now*, Joe, don't you get?"

At that moment her cell rang. It lay on a side table next to the sofa. Sliding away from Joe, she picked it up, smiled when she saw the name and took the call.

"Oh, hi David. You given that proposition of mine from yesterday any further thought yet? .... Sure, I have plenty time to answer some of your concerns, I would be happy to meet with you later tonight if you would like," Amelia trailed off in a conversation with David turning her back on Joe.

She heard the door to the suite slam shut, smiled, and relaxed into a large oversized chair kicking off her heels.

"Now, what did you say about those annual business reports again David?"

During the six months Joe was entangled with Amelia, Ashley found him withdrawn and distracted. He had little interest in going with her to any pre birthing classes, and he spent a great deal of time locked away in his den. He also would flit off overnight without warning rambling on about some huge impending deal, and upon his return lock himself up again behind closed doors. On occasion she would find Joe on the floor playing with Joe, Jr. and his fire engines.

Ashley felt huge, her belly growing, and although prone to hysterical emotional attacks, which she always blamed on her hormonal imbalance, she largely ignored Joe's disinterest, and wrote it off to his being overly busy, and the sight of her not too physically attractive body, off putting. The rest of the time she spent busying herself in preparation for the new baby.

Then one night, right before the birth of Madison Joe came back from a business trip particularly moody. He became angry at the slightest of things, refused to eat, and if he wasn't locked up in his den, he was at the gym. Pam and her friends fabricated the reason to be one of unconscious transference. They all remembered this from Psych 101 class. Ashley was unconsciously transferring her hormonal imbalance issues onto Joe, and he was acting out on them. Pam remembered the same behavior in John, and it annoyed her to no end, she said. But, after the baby is born, they reassured her, everything would return to normal, including the sex.

Pam was right of course. A few weeks after the birth of Madison Joe returned to his usual demanding sex drive. In fact, their sex life improved considerably. She wasn't sure if Joe had secretly signed up for sex classes, but if he did, they better have included no practice tries, or reading *A Lovers Guide to the Kama Sutra*. Regardless, she didn't question his robust need. It made her feel in demand and loved all over again. They would go out with friends, have wonderful dinners, and return to have extraordinary sex all over the house.

∞∞

The Palm Oasis was just as its name suggested, a haven, a retreat, a sanctuary, except rather than being a retreat for all things good and healthy, it was a hot bed for pure gossip. Obviously, having such a temptation it was the most popular hair salon in town, and its shampooers, stylists, and colorists were addicted to its reputation, all the while claiming how they detested the mere concept of talking about and judging others. But that was all they did, from Tuesday through Saturday.

Penny Choo would come in wearing a new pair of yellow platforms, and the hairstylists would all gather around her, and marvel at the beauty and the fine taste their client displayed.

A little later, while mixing Penny Choo's exotic new hair color, for her new doo, the overtly feminine colorist, Stephen, would converse with the other colorists, and in a mocking and disparaging tone go on a rant.

"What do you think was going through her head buying those yellow shoes? That girl has no idea how to buy 'fuck me' shoes! Poor thing, but then if you *only* knew her mother, you could understand *exactly* why she doesn't have a clue. Clueless! Some of these women, totally clueless! *All* the money in the world, and *no clue* how to spend it! I should only have their money to throw around in the fashion world, Aaah a dream! What a dream!" The last statement always emphasized by the colorist waving his arms in the air.

He would then announce, "off to apply color to Penny Choo's hair, and it won't be blond! Ha! Ha! Ha!"

Amelia would always pay a visit to the Palm Oasis when in town. However, today she made a special point of stopping by there. She had Elizabeth schedule a hair cut, color and blow dry with her usual master colorist, and stylist there. Henry, was her all time favorite gossip monger. He firmly believed he never wished anyone any harm, and all he ever did was keep people abreast of the happenings around town. Henry was a raving queen, and Amelia appreciated his hugely artistic flair.

She always gave Henry a whopping tip, encouraging him to spill the beans at the slightest provocation, and most of the time this really needed to be ever so slight. And of course, Henry loved Amelia.

"Amelia, Darling, how have you been? How's the fashion world in Paris?" Henry would press Amelia for information, while shuffling her off to his private hair cutting station.

"Oh, and I want your opinion on something Darling, I had the most interesting client the other day, she had just returned from Prague, and she said…." And, so off Henry would go as if suffering from verbal diarrhea.

Henry craved to have Amelia to himself. It gave him the opportunity to hear all the trendy news first, and then place him in great demand with the others. There was a male in particular Henry loved to keep in suspense, Kyle. Ever since Kyle joined the Palm Oasis colorist team a year ago, Henry became obsessed with him. It was Kyle this, and Kyle that, Kyle please give me your most honest opinion, Kyle you look absolutely radiant today,… Kyle, Kyle, Kyle.

Kyle on the other hand, had his eye on Sable, a super cute Cuban guy with a small round butt, deep brown eyes with extraordinarily long, and thick eyelashes, as Kyle would describe Sable when his name was mentioned.

However, Sable had his eye on Simon who refused to date anyone from work no matter how absolutely *over the top* drop dead gorgeous they may be, after all principles were principles. Although, there had been some gossip going around once, that Simon got totally smashed one night at a club, and someone saw Sable driving him home, his head lying gently on Sable's shoulder. But there was no follow up to this innocuous story, and so, the circle of love continued to go around and around at the Palm Oasis.

"Darling," started Amelia as she sat in Henry's hair cutting chair, "do you know an Ashley Loveit?"

"Oh, my God, do I know an Ashley Loveit! Of course! She has hair to die for, the cutest bod, superb dress sense, just love it! Ha, Ha, Haw! Get it Amel, Love it, and Loveit?" Henry responded in his usual excitable way.

He was also the only one who called Amelia, Amel, no one else had this privilege.

"But you know, she doesn't have the nicest husband. I mean he is to die for also, wouldn't say *no* if he was offering, you know what I mean, but such a womanizer. Seen him with *my own eyes*," Henry said patting Amelia's right shoulder with a black comb, to emphasize his point. "But that poor little girl has no clue. Even her friends talk about it here. Just ask Kyle," Henry continued to scandal.

"Well, Henry Darling, you see the thing is, I knew her husband some time ago, but I haven't spoken to him in years, and you know I would feel really awkward calling him up out of the blue, but I actually wanted to get in touch with Ashley. You see here is his number in my cell phone." Luckily Amelia hadn't erased Joe's number just yet, even though it had been a few years since she last saw him.

"He gave me his wife's number and I must have erased it when I upgraded cell phones, and I'm only in town tonight," she said not telling the entire truth, "and I really, really, really need to speak to her. Do you think you could just look it up for me? Please, please Henry, just for me, your old time favorite client?" Amelia said, turning on the charm full blast.

As usual, her reputation unfailing, no man ever able to refuse her, Henry said in a whisper, "Well, okay, but if she asks you where you got it, you never got it from me, you got that Amel?"

Amelia smiled, nodded, and then added, "I did tell you I once had it, I just seemed to have dropped it when I got my phone updated. But my lips are sealed. Oh, and Henry I would like you to add an extra mane of hair with a good deal of extensions," Amelia said, racking up her bill, which translated into a much higher tip for Henry.

"Amel, for you I will kill da bull!" Henry exclaimed, his mind already racing with options of how he anticipated spending his tip.

Amelia was disinterested in the size of her bill, all she cared about was to be utterly sure her head of hair wouldn't be upstaged by Ashley Loveit's.

∞∞

Amelia called Ashley the following morning. Ashley was feeling good that morning, and in her car about to go out and look for a cute new summer outfit for Amber. Amber had been invited to a birthday party at the Woodfield Suburban Clubhouse.

"Hi, Ashley my name is Amelia Swift. You've never met me but I knew your husband a few years back, and he gave me your number. Is this a good time to talk?"

"Well, yeah, I'm sorry what did you say your name was again?" Ashley said, caught off guard.

"Amelia Swift."

Being in a rather happy mood, and with unusually little set on her agenda that day she agreed to meet Amelia, "Where do you want to meet?" Ashley asked.

"Well, there is this Italian Bistro called Verona's on Ocean Drive, would that work for you?" Amelia asked trying to be accommodating. Ashley knew Verona's. It was an intimate little restaurant with a very select menu, and an even more select clientele.

"So, how do I know what you look like?" Ashley asked the most logical question.

"When you go in, ask to be seated at my table – Amelia Swift. I will call ahead and reserve one. 12:30 good for you?"

"Yes," agreed Ashley and she picked up a pen she always kept handy in her car, and jotted down the details.

Ashley had no idea what this was all about. But she couldn't call any of her friends for fear of alerting them to something she may not be aware of. Moreover, there seemed little which could shock her now after Joe. So, she decided to just keep it to herself, and stay calm. She had begun some meditation to help her learn how to remain calm and focused.

At 12:28 Ashley entered Verona's Italian Bistro. She announced she was the guest of Amelia Swift, and the host welcomed her and seated her at a small round table in a rather remote area of the restaurant. The host was rapidly followed by the Maitre d' who animatedly introduced himself and welcomed her as the guest of Ms. Amelia Swift, and asked if she required a bartender to take her drink order. Ashley declined, after thanking him.

At 12:33 Amelia Swift entered Verona's Italian Bistro. She was clad in a beautiful black and red soft flowing dress. The upper half well tailored exposing her beautifully rounded breasts, the waist pulled in tight, the skirt somewhat flared, and just the right length to indicate she was a woman with beautiful legs. Her legs ended in a pair of slim looking black shoes with an elegant and sophisticated black rose with red trim planted at its tip. Her purse was slim and sleek and hung over her left shoulder. It had the same rose nestled on the clasp as her shoes. Ashley could tell this was a woman with superb clothes and shoe sense. She did love her head of hair, but was sure there were a good amount of extensions in it.

Amelia entered the restaurant with a great deal of pomp and grandeur. The Maitre d' ran up to her the moment she entered the establishment taking her hand and kissing it.

"Oh, Ms. Swift it is an absolute pleasure to see you again. I do hope the weather in New York has improved. We have your usual table, as you requested. Over there your guest is already seated. Is there anything I can get for you Ms. Swift?" the Maitre d' continued to gush.

"Oh, no thank you Tony. Just lead me to my table that is all," Amelia responded respectfully.

"Yes, Ms. Swift. But of course."

Upon arriving at the table, Amelia put her hand out to shake Ashley's and introduced herself.

"Thank you for meeting me Ashley," she said.

Ashley was just as Henry had described her, except much more beautiful. She had a natural beauty which glowed as well, and she was really quite poised. Ashley never responded to Amelia's words. She just sat taking in all that Amelia was, beautiful, elegant and graceful. It made Ashley feel a little inadequate.

Amelia sat down, and a drink she never ordered was placed in front of her.

"Would you like something to drink Ashley?" she asked in a pleasant tone as the bartender stood beside them.

"A Perrier thank you." The bartender then rushed off leaving an awkward silence.

"This is a very pretty restaurant. I have lived here a long time and never tried it," Ashley said.

"Yes, it is a lovely place, and the food is equally as good," Amelia said continuing the small talk.

Ashley was becoming increasingly uneasy.

"Please let me order for you, Ashley, if you don't mind. I really know what their specialties are here." Amelia said trying to be helpful, but Ashley found it a little bossy. Nevertheless, Ashley waved her approval.

"Would you prefer fish, meat or chicken?" Amelia asked.

"Well, none actually, I'm beginning this plant-based diet, and I would rather stick to vegetables and salads, if that's ok," Ashley deep down enjoyed giving out this instruction to complicate matters, although, she wasn't quite sure why she felt competitive with this woman. She had never met her until now, and Amelia hadn't said anything to offend her...yet.

Amelia on the other hand was already beginning to like Ashley, and was more than happy to stick to a plant-based lunch, after all it reminded her of her beloved Sri Lanka.

"Well, in that case we'll take this one," and she pointed to the menu. "Thank you Tony, and to begin with this," she pointed again at the menu. "Oh, and Tony, please, we don't want to be disturbed," Amelia commanded.

"Absolutely, Ms. Swift. Absolutely, I understand completely."

While Amelia opened her napkin and placed it across her lap, Tony loosened the ties to the curtains on either side of their table and drew them closed, as if drawing the drapes to a large window, and with that the Maitre d' and the rest of the restaurant disappeared, leaving Ashley and Amelia totally alone. Ashley began to feel as if she was trapped on the inside of a walnut shell.

The two women stared facing one another.

"So, you said you know Joe?" Ashley said, feeling a little uncomfortable with their total isolation.

"Yes," Amelia said, "but I have something to tell you, and for the first time in my life not quite sure how to say this," Amelia said. "You see Ashley, it is not my intention to hurt you, I don't even know you, but some years ago, I met Joe, and we, well, we…" Amelia just could not finish the sentence. In all her years she had never been at a loss for words, but at this moment sitting across from this woman, she was.

"You slept with my husband, is that what you trying to say?" Ashley finished the sentence looking directly at her.

"Well, yes," said Amelia.

"Well," said Ashley, "you weren't the first one he cheated on me with," Ashley retorted not enjoying this at all.

Then she said, "But answer me this Amelia, how long ago exactly was this?" surprising Amelia.

"About four years ago," Amelia answered.

"Four years ago, and you call me out of the blue to tell me about something that happened four years ago?" Ashley asked a little irritated.

"Not exactly," answered Amelia.

Ashley stared right back at Amelia. She knew exactly what was coming next, and she was not prepared for it at all, and she knew it.

"Ashley," continued Amelia, "I have a child, Joe's child."

Ashley then began to laugh, she wondered just how many of Joe's children were actually out there running around. Amelia didn't join her.

"My daughter's name is Ashley," Amelia added trying to be heard above her laughter. "Well, that was a perfect name you chose Amelia!" Ashley managed to spew out in-between her laughter.

"But that's not the reason why I called to meet you here today, Ashley," Amelia said still pressing on.

"What else could there be Amelia, that you have two of Joe's children running around!" And with that Ashley burst out laughing again.

"Ashley, I realize this must all be a shock to you, but…" Amelia tried to continue, but Ashley was still laughing.

Their starters arrived, and Ashley's laughter seemed to be infectious, making both servers smile too. Amelia, however, was not that jovial. The servers then left after asking if there was anything else they might need.

Ashley tried to calm down and compose herself.

"So, what made you choose the name Ashley for your daughter?" Ashley asked, and then again just couldn't contain herself and burst out laughing.

Amelia began to eat her food. She was not quite sure what to make of Ashley.

"Look," said Ashley, casually nibbling on a lettuce leaf, "I am in the process of divorcing Joe. It's getting messy, and he is actually fighting me to be the primary parent. We have two children together. Under Florida law there is no such thing as one parent having custody of the children, it is a shared custody kind of concept where you have a primary parent where the children live most of the time, and then there is a secondary parent where the children usually go every other weekend, and one night a week. I'm not quite sure how he plans on pulling this one off though, I mean he is clearly in another relationship with a Mel or Melanie, or whatever her name is. The strange thing is he was the one who asked for the divorce, but had I known what I know today, I would have asked for it ages ago," Ashley said still enjoying her food, "This is good," she added pointing at her salad plate.

"Four years ago you said, actually that was around when I was pregnant with Madison. Oh, I remember, he must have been seeing you then because he was acting so strangely, but I was so pregnant I just thought it was my hormones going crazy. Yeah, I remember now. Well, if it is any consolation he must have really been in love with you because he was pretty much a bear to live with for some time," Ashley continued casually, thinking thank heavens I meditated before meeting this one.

Then Ashley thought how strange this meeting with Amelia seemed, she would never talk so freely like this with anyone, well other than Lily of course. Perhaps it's this walnut shell hiding us from the world making me feel safe to talk, she thought.

"Look Ashley, I'm going to file for child support from Joe. I wanted to let you know ahead of time, I didn't want you to find out after, you know, when he got served. I had no idea you were divorcing him, and I didn't want the process server serving him at his home, and you not know anything about this. I don't need his money, but I want him to acknowledge his child. I want the paternity test done. Not for me, I have no claim on Joe, but I don't want my daughter not knowing her father. I want to allow her the opportunity whether they connect later when she is older or not. He may be a crappy husband but perhaps he may be a decent father."

Amelia continued, "This was a big decision for me to make because I really was very done with Joe. I just didn't anticipate this. It was only after Ashley started to grow up I realized this decision may not have been mine to make. I like to be in control but not controlling. I hope you understand."

"I appreciate that Amelia, actually I really do. I guess the process serving won't be much of a problem. He's living with his mother though, and I will happily give you her address," Ashley responded, then she thought of something.

"Amelia, by the way, will you give me enough time to inform my lawyer about this. There may be a timing issue here, and I would appreciate it, if you would work the service of process with my case. I mean it shouldn't affect your case at all, it just may turn out quite beneficial for me, and my children that's all," Ashley said, surprising Amelia at how agile her mind was.

Amelia could clearly relate to the scheming and planning intellect of the female species, and so happily responded, "Yes, I think that would be in order. I haven't settled on a Florida lawyer here yet, so we have a little time."

Ashley then added, "Amelia, if you plan on hiring a Florida lawyer mine is one of the best in the area you may want to do a 'child support interview' with him, you wouldn't want Joe hiring him, although come to think of it, I don't think Andy can take your case because that would create a conflict of interest for him, Andy that's my lawyer, Andy Gold, because he knows too much about me. Not sure though, come to think of it, if the money was right I wouldn't trust Andy getting around the Florida Bar ethics rules," Ashley rambled.

Then once again on high alert Ashley said to Amelia, "why don't you give me your personal information Amelia that way I can reach you as need be."

Amelia passed Ashley her business card. They both smiled broadly. Ashley, feeling proud of herself for finally thinking outside the box, and Amelia loving the concept of being part of another scheme.

Their respective lunch entrees arrived, and both women ate with great relish, their minds spinning with excitement. While they ate they were left to their own personal thoughts.

Have I just joined forces with my husband's concubine? Ashley asked herself.

I really appreciate Ashley's creative insight here, and her real desire to possess and protect her children, Amelia thought. I think I had underestimated our Ms. Ashley. She is a lot more savy than I anticipated, and certainly not the crumbling housewife I expected.

This could just be what I need to finally be done with Joe and his mother, Ashley thought. She briefly raised her eyes to the heavens, and said, thank you God.

Things were playing out a little differently in Amelia's head, you see Amelia, and Amelia alone knew the real reason she had stuck her neck out so far today, something she couldn't admit to anyone but herself: She loved her daughter Ashley more than life itself, and would do whatever it took to make her life better than Amelia's was growing up.

Both woman shook hands in the parking lot, this time on a more equal footing, and a tiny bit less secretive. Ashley reached into her purse for her cell phone and put a call into Andy Gold.

He was impressed with Ashley, "Ashley, I think you may just have brought home the gold, my little wise alchemist."

Chapter NINE

A s time passed Ashley found herself living in different realities.

A couple of weeks after Lily had dropped Ari off at Ashley's home, Lily called Ashley. She wanted to be sure Ashley had returned some balance to her life. She was happy to find Ashley sounded more upbeat, even though she was in the midst of a divorce war. She let Lily know about all the exciting breakthroughs she had begun to experience as she surrendered her *victimhood* mentality. Lily was thrilled to hear of Ashley's change of heart. It was also at this point Lily suggested a few books for Ashley to read, like, *The Wisdom* of William James, Mother Teresa's, *A Simple* Path, and *The Art of Happiness*, an interview of the Dalai Lama by Howard Cutler, M.D. She felt it would help her cope better with all the anguish and stress the divorce process was triggering.

She also strongly suggested Ashley begin to pray again, as she opened her eyes to the world in the morning, and right before she shut them at night. Say a prayer for humanity Ashley, there is so much we can accomplish through prayer. Bless the divorce process, bless the lawyers, and bless the judge. Prayer is a very powerful tool. Ashley realized she had not prayed in years. While God had not left her life entirely, she only seemed to engage that energy when she was ranting on about one personal issue or another, other than this, she had for years largely blocked herself off from the Universe, long forgetting its magic.

Now, every day Ashley took time out to find some morsel of inner peace. She bought the books Lily suggested, and one by one, began to read them. She also returned to prayer as Lily suggested, and returned to painting, allowing the paint brush to whisk her away into another world. Ashley was beginning to be re-introduced to a different side of herself, and it felt comfortable, very comfortable.

"We all know about this Ashley, we just loose our way sometimes," Lily had said. "It is time to change the way you think. Time to approach your life from a more curious or inquisitive mind set, and find out who Ashley is and what Ashley wants out of life. Start to let go Ashley and let God. You are not in control, you just deluded into thinking you are. It is time to begin to trust again. Trust in what is happening in your life and the outcomes. When we think we are what others want us to be and then find they don't feel that way about us we feel as if we aren't anymore. This is misguiding yourself. Only your ego wants you to believe you are what others believe you to be, for your 'ego' works from fear. Fear will make you cling to everything and anything. It blinds you. It blinds you into thinking you need something when you really don't. We are not our clothes, our cars, our homes, nor the image of what others want us to be. This is not our true nature. It is time to find your true nature. Change is always uncomfortable at first, but we should all get used to it because it is very constant in our lives, and this is a good thing not a bad thing."

Aside from the spiritual world, Ashley also lived in another world. A practical material one. One, pressing her to attend to more realistic, earthly, and mundane matters, like her divorce from Joe. This world included lawyers, depositions, court hearings, and the like.

And, then there was Ashley's friend's world. A world, totally unaware of either of her other two worlds. Her friends had no idea about her immersion in the spiritual realm, and equally no idea about her practical realistic one either. She still hadn't told them about her divorce. While it was easy to determine Ashley's friend's world was not a spiritual one, it started to become apparent to Ashley, her friend's world didn't quite fit the practical realistic Earthly plane either! Especially, after Ashley received a phone call like this one from Pam.

"Hi, Ash. How you doing?" Pam asked, acting delighted to finally reach Ashley but not truly interested in listening to her response. She had something much more exciting to get off her chest.

"Listen, Ash. Tay, Amber and I were chatting with Tay's step daughter, Sami, you know the one whose 17? She is really cute, you should see her. Well, anyway, she showed us this adorable tattoo she just had done on her foot. We all loved it. We spent hours chatting about tattoos and our bodies afterwards, you would have loved it, and here's what we decided: We would declare tomorrow 'National Woodfield Womens' Body Day!' And get this, to celebrate, we all decided to get a tattoo!! Yes, all of us, Ash!! Can you believe it?"

Ashley couldn't respond. All she could think was, and this is how I used to occupy my time.

"Ash, you still there?" Pam added, concerned her cell phone had dropped the call.

"Yes, Pam, I'm still here," Ashley answered flatly.

Pam, oblivious to Ashley's disinterest continued, "I'm going to have one on my hip, really, really low near my panty line. Amber wants one on her lower back, and Tay is going to go with Sami's idea, on her foot. We would love you to come Ash. You should ask Joe where he would like you to have one, Ash. We were all talking about asking you to come with us, you're always up for everything. Won't you come with us, Ash, please, please!! Sami told us of this really safe tattoo artist place we can go to. She said we must be careful where we go, we don't want to pick up any diseases."

"Pam, I think I'm going to pass on this one," Ashley said, smiling to herself.

"But why Ash, you know tattooing has become the latest form of body art, and it's no longer confined to military dudes or rebels," said Pam.

"Sami told you that?" Asked Ashley rhetorically, "because you sound like an infomercial Pam."

"Oh, Ash, I must tell you something else," Pam continued with equal excitement totally ignoring Ashley's insult, "I bumped into that crazy back neighbor of mine, you know the one that takes her dog everywhere, that tiny little snappy creature, you know the one, Nicole? Well, get this, she told me when I bumped into her at the *Sequel* she was taking her Timmy, that's the name of that nasty unfriendly little miniature terrier of hers, to a,... get this Pam, a d-o-g plastic surgeon!!! Yes, a Dr. Schnauzer, have you ever heard of such a thing? A dog plastic surgeon!! Well, I just don't know how I didn't burst out laughing in her face. She told me she thinks his nose is off center for the breed. Oh, my G-d! How off the wall is that?"

Then without waiting for a response she said, "Okay well, I will tell the girls I asked Ash. Got to run. Nail filler appointment, bye."

No, Ashley could no longer find a planet in her life which might possibly accommodate this kind of recreational mentality.

∞∞

The day of Joe's deposition Ashley woke early. She tried to meditate, although it proved difficult to focus. She listened to some meditative CD's and then went to get herself ready. She dressed slowly applying her makeup methodically. When she arrived at the deposition she looked radiant, Andy reassured her.

He knew this was going to be a tough one for her today, and tried to reassure her everything was going to be fine. She needed to remember not to allow anything he said get under her skin because it was imperative he stay completely focused all through the deposition, he didn't want to have to stop because she couldn't control her emotions.

"Thank heavens you're not my therapist," Ashley told him, and they both laughed.

Joe looked his usual handsome self. He was looking slimmer in his customary Hugo Boss wardrobe, and a little tanned. Maybe this Mel was good for him, Ashley thought. She then realized this was the most *detaching from Joe* remark she had made to date.

Joe was sworn in and then asked to state his name for the record.

"Joseph Jake Loveit," he said clearly.

Andy Gold was grueling. He questioned Joe on every microscopic detail of his life, from his childhood to present day. Steve Silver desperately tried to make effective objections here and there. Each time Steve objected, Andy mockingly, reminding the court reporter to simply certify that aspect of the record for the court so they could proceed. Time was money, he would say. Which, incidentally, was also taken down as part of the record.

It became very uncomfortable for Ashley emotionally when Andy broached the subject of Joe's infidelity. Joe, on the other hand, seemed unaffected having to reveal this side of himself.

"Mr. Loveit, in all the years you were married how many times did you sleep with another woman? And please let me clarify this here to help you answer correctly, I mean if you slept with one women ten times, you would still count her as one woman," Andy Gold asked in a disdainful tone, in anticipation of what Joe was about to say. Andy's private investigator had done a substantial amount of home work on Joe.

Joe was about to answer when, Steve Silver butted in, "Objection, this has nothing to do with what's best for the children." Joe closed his mouth, confused. He had nothing to hide.

"Counselor, I do not care about how moral or immoral Mr. Loveit's personal life may be. The issue is, if Mr. Loveit has a habitual tendency to sleep with women on a whim then how do we know he will be able to be there when the children need him, he may live a very unsettling lifestyle for children?" Andy pointed out. Joe shifted in his chair, Andy Gold had a point. But Joe had a solution, he'd hire a sleep in nanny.

Andy turned back to face Joe directing him, and rousing him from his daze, "Please answer the question Mr. Loveit. If you have forgotten what I asked you I would be happy to have the court reporter read it back to you."

"I don't remember how many," Joe said his eyes not anywhere in Ashley's direction. Ashley shifted in her chair, yearning, but at the same time *not* desiring to hear Joe's response. What was it with Joe, even in the hot seat, he looked handsome. Truly handsome.

"Well, was it once or more than once?" Andy Gold continued to pursue his line of questioning.

Ashley began to twirl a pen around, and around between her fingers, her eyes fixed on Joe. Andy cleared his throat. That was a signal to Ashley. She placed the pen down in front of her.

"More than once," Joe said. Okay Ashley could account for Amelia, and Mel.

"Was it twice or more than twice?" Andy Gold pushed even further.

"More than twice," Joe responded. Ashley's lower jaw began to slowly separate from the upper one.

"Was it three times or more than three times?

"Objection, you are absolutely splitting hairs here counselor, this is ridiculous," Steve Silver started raising his voice, all being caught on video tape.

Andy Gold realizing, "Counselor, you may want to tone down a little, the video is still running."

"You are being absolutely preposterous!" Steve Silver continued in a much lower tone.

Ignoring him and looking back at Joe, Andy Gold pressed on: "Please answer the question Mr. Loveit."

"More than three times," Joe answered without hesitation sitting back in his chair.

"Would it be reasonable to assume Mr. Loveit that you slept with other woman more than eight times during your marriage to Mrs. Loveit?"

"Yes," answered Joe, not feeling in the slightest way concerned about what he was saying, after all, Ashley had thrown him out, what did he care. They could shine all the lights they wanted on him. He was going to tell it how it is.

Ashley got up slowly, and left the room. She really didn't want to hear anymore. She felt like a total idiot. A dumbo, a stupid, stupid, out of touch housewife. Joe didn't look at her, his gaze remained on Andy Gold, nor did anyone else look at Ashley for that matter, they were all focused on Joe.

As Andy Gold was about to determine Mr. Loveit's betrayal was so numerous he could not list the names of all the females he had slept with over the past few years, an earsplitting scream was heard coming through the wall right behind where Joe was sitting. Unbeknown to everyone in the room the wall behind Joe separated the deposition conference room from the ladies restroom.

All that was heard was a female's voice yelling, "Shit you fucking, fucking, fucking stupid, stupid, idiot, where the fuck have you been these past seven years?" Not necessarily an unusual vocal to hear on this floor, considering it was frequently used to house family law depositions.

Then there was this tremendous thumping on the wall behind Joe, once, twice, three, four times, THUD, THUD,

~ 165 ~

THUD, THUD. The entire wall behind Joe vibrated, and the doors to the cabinet which sat in front of it, rattled and shook as if they were in the midst of an earthquake. Everyone in the room sat dead still, the court reporter stopped typing, and set her hands down in her lap, no one said a word. At that moment the identification of the woman became known, "Is there any woman left in this fucking world that you didn't fuck you fucking lying idiot Joe Loveit?" Still no one said anything. They all sat, waiting for it to stop, and strangely it did, as randomly as it had begun.

Ashley re-entered the room. While her facial expression appeared calm, her appearance was a little rumpled, her shirt tail was hanging out below one side of her jacket, her hair untidy, and she appeared to be limping. No one said a word. It seemed some aspect of her pain had been clearly understood by all, except Joe of course, but then again, he never understood the idea of pain, except when a stock lost value on the New York Stock Exchange.

As she resumed her seat, Andy Gold leaned over to her and asked gently, "Are you feeling better dear?"

"A hundred times better, thank you Andy for asking. Please proceed," Ashley replied completely calmly. Andy couldn't resist a smile, compared to any of his other clients he found Ashley's method of releasing her emotions unmatched, and her timing, like an Andy Gold exclusive, he thought.

The rest of the deposition unfolded with no more debut performances from Ashley. Instead she developed a thick skin, and even began to make a few sideline jokes to herself when Joe would answer Andy's questions. Andy let these all pass.

Andy asked Joe how many hours a week he felt he worked.

"At least seventy to eighty hours a week," he replied.

Not including your fuck time Joe? Ashley mumbled under her breath.

"Are you presently in a relationship Mr. Loveit? Andy Gold asked.

"Yes, I am," Joe answered proudly.

Sure you are darling, you can't let Mr. Penis down now can you? He's a needy little business associate isn't he?

"Where does she reside Mr. Loveit?" Andy asked

"New York," Joe said

"Do you get to see her often?" was Andy's question for Joe.

"As much as I can. I work a lot in New York. Leave the kids with my mother," Joe volunteered more than he needed, he just wanted out of there.

And in her mind, Oh, yes, your lovely upstanding citizen mother.

"Do you plan on moving to New York Mr. Loveit?" Andy asked.

"Yes, once all this is behind me," Joe answered smiling.

And again in her mind, Oh, how much you pine for your life here with your kids, you stupid son-of-a-bitch!

Ashley sat up in her chair, she suddenly realized something, that is exactly what he is; a stupid son-of-a-bitch. She started to giggle, there is some truth in that statement after all. Thank you, whoever you were who invented that one! Nice! She thought.

"How would you plan on arranging for the children to see their mother?" Andy asked.

Andy Gold continued his deposition with Joe for several hours, building steadily Ashley's case as to why Joe was not the ideal primary parent for the children. And by the sound of it, not the primary choice husband either.

But Joe did confirm the numbers Andy Gold's forensic accountant determined, and Joe was quite proud and open to express it. Joe had built a sizeable sum of money during the marriage, and was willing to share it with Ashley. He would just make more, is how he saw it.

Andy Gold as anticipated, was quite sure from this deposition, Joe really wasn't concerned about being the primary parent, his mother was, she had it in for Ashley. Mrs.

Patterson had it in for the whole world, Ashley was just a by product of it, he realized.

But, Andy Gold really needed one more piece of information against Joe to seal this case, and walk away with the prize. He wasn't sure what it was a few days ago, but he was sure it would come to him, once he reviewed a copy of the taped video deposition with the psychologist.

It turned out, Andy Gold didn't need the psychologist for his case clincher, because a little while later Amelia Swift stepped into the big picture.

Andy Gold and Amelia Swift hit it off immediately, probably because Andy had no romantic intentions towards Amelia, and Amelia was a client of Verona's, an old time favorite haunt of his. Amelia was also in search of a lawyer referral, and knew whoever Andy Gold recommended would be one of the best. Andy would have referred Steve Silver under normal circumstances, but Steve would probably get a second case out of Joe anyway, having to represent him next against Amelia.

Andy briefly discussed Amelia's relevance in Ashley's case, and Amelia promptly agreed to be of assistance. Mary Weeks was instructed to expeditiously draft an amendment to the Witness List in Ashley's case, adding Amelia's name. Shortly thereafter, and as predicted, Steve Silver requested to take Amelia's deposition. He definitely needed to hear what this witness had to say, and he wondered what performance Ashley would pull this time.

However, Andy Gold had some kind of heart, contrary to all those who ever opposed him. When Amelia's deposition was set he called up Ashley to notify her that she really needn't be present at the deposition. Ashley found herself not too distraught, and used the time to relax and take the children to the latest Disney movie release. He also informed Mary Weeks and his intern he would be attending the deposition alone.

When Steve Silver discovered Ashley wasn't going to be present at the deposition he felt a little sad, "What no showdown today, Andy?" he said.

Andy just smiled at Steve. Oh, there was going to be a show down alright today, just not what you're expecting that's all, can't use the same act now can we? Andy thought haughtily to himself.

Next to Steve sat Joe, as anticipated by Andy and Amelia. Joe was well turned-out as usual but not in his customary Hugo Boss. Today, he wore a pale blue Swedish Eton shirt, Italian bamboo silk pants, and a pair of finely crafted shoes from the Amedeo Testoni line. A magnificent shoe, Andy couldn't help but notice. Andy was unsure whether Joe's change in style was for Amelia or a Mel's influence.

Amelia was sworn in and Steve Silver did a very thorough questioning of Amelia and her role in Joe's life. Three hours later, Andy was given the opportunity to ask some questions of his own.

Joe had been listening with half an ear while his lawyer deposed Amelia. He still had the 'hots' for her. And today she looked hot, he thought, but he had Mel, and she was hot as hell. He wasn't quite sure why his lawyer needed him here today, and he was hoping he could get out soon and *that* 'sparkle pants,' Andy Gold over there, didn't need to take up too much more of his time.

"Ms. Swift you said earlier your relationship with the petitioner Mr. Loveit lasted about six months, is that correct?" Andy Gold asked her.

"Yes," she responded.

"On what days and times of day was it that you and Mr. Loveit would meet?" Andy asked.

"Oh, various times and days. It depended on my schedule. It could be a Monday night, a Tuesday morning, a Wednesday evening, A Friday afternoon, a Saturday night, Sunday morning, really no set time." She answered.

"And for how many hours would you spend together on those occasions?" He asked.

"Anywhere from about four to twenty four and on occasion forty eight hours," she answered honestly. Joe looked up at Amelia and smiled broadly. Amelia didn't notice she was focused on Andy Gold.

"And tell me Ms. Swift in all those six months when he was in your company did he call home to speak with his son, Joe, Jr. ever?" Andy Gold asked. Joe's smile faded, and he looked down at the blank notepad before him.

"Never," Amelia answered looking over at Joe. Joe's eyes remained on the notepad.

"Never at one time did he say he needed to call home to speak with Joe, Jr.?" Andy confirmed.

"Asked and answered, this is badgering," Steve Silver added.

"Humor me Ms. Swift, one more time," Andy Gold said sarcastically.

"Never," answered Amelia.

"Did he ever talk about his son?" Andy Gold asked.

"He may have mentioned him briefly once or twice, but not much more than that," she responded.

"So, let me get this straight, in the entire six months you were having an affair with Mr. Loveit, he only mentioned his son once or twice, but not much more than that?" Andy Gold kept going.

"Yes," Amelia answered.

"Ms. Swift at the time you were having an affair with Mr. Loveit did you know his wife was pregnant with their second child?" Andy Gold brought up.

Joe stretched his legs out before him, and leaned back in his chair. Enough already about the kid's stuff, he thought to himself, irritated.

"Only towards the end, the last week or so," Amelia said.

Andy Gold fulfilled Joe's wish, and changed the subject, "You said earlier Mr. Loveit wanted to leave his wife and go off with you, do you recall what his exact words were when he said that?"

"Yes, as a matter of fact I do because they shocked me so much," she said.

"Can you tell us exactly what you recall him saying?" asked Andy Gold. Joe shifted again in his seat, and leaned to the left. He propped his head up with his left arm, picked up a pen, and began to doodle on the pad before him, tuning out Amelia's deposition.

"He said, I'll leave Ashley. I don't love her. I only married her because all the guys I knew thought she was hot, and they all wanted her. I could come and live with you, and travel wherever you go. I only need a laptop to do my work. That's what he said," Amelia responded very eloquently.

"So, you rejected him, Ms. Swift?" asked Andy enjoying himself as he usually did in depositions, and especially today.

"Yes, I didn't love him," Amelia said warmly falling into step with Andy Gold.

"Ms. Swift you said earlier you had one child, a little girl?" Andy Gold asked.

"Yes," she answered smiling.

"Did Mr. Loveit know your daughter?" asked Andy Gold. Joe tuned back into the proceedings, without looking at Amelia. He continued to doodle, he had to keep himself awake somehow.

"No," Amelia said.

"Why is that Ms. Swift, why did Mr. Loveit not get to meet your daughter?" Andy pressed, waiting, waiting, waiting, for Amelia's debut.

Amelia sat upright in her chair and in a very loud and clear voice looking directly at Joe she answered, "because my daughter is Joe Loveit's child, and was born after we had parted ways."

Joe almost fell on his face as his left arm slipped from under his chin. What the fuck! He thought.

Steve Silver jumped up out of his seat, "Objection, objection, objection…"

"Yes?" Andy Gold said smiling, and turning to Steve Silver, and in a very slow and controlled tone added, "What's the objection counselor?"

"There is no proof that Ms. Swif, Mrs Swif, …Ms. Swift's child is my client's child!" Steve Silver managed to blurt out.

"So, noted," said Andy Gold casually. And he turned back to Amelia.

Joe was now on full alert.

"Ms. Swift, are you sure that Joe Loveit is the father of your child?" Andy Gold asked, in Heaven at this point. These were the kind of moments Andy Gold dreamed of in a case.

"Yes," Amelia responded.

"How do you know this?" Andy holding onto all the drama as long as he could, he was still a true actor at heart.

"He was the only man I slept with for that six month period," she said looking back at Joe.

Joe's facial color left his face, with all his enthusiasm to leave. He felt stuck to his chair. He suddenly felt very hot, and confined. He needed air. He unbuttoned the top button of his shirt.

Moments later Andy Gold concluded his redirect of Amelia.

Steve Silver still visibly in shock, and a little confused as to exactly what kind of lifestyle his client Joe Loveit had actually been living, decided it best to quickly, officially end the entire deposition without going too deeply into the child paternity issue. He would first need to consult with his client regarding this matter, because this line of questioning could prove to be a double edged sword for Joe, so instead he reserved the right to recall Amelia. Andy Gold certainly had no objection to that one.

Steve's client wasn't making it any easier on him either, Joe was shuffling excessively in his chair and cursing to himself under his breath.

The moment Steve Silver released Amelia from the court ordered deposition she sent a text message. Everyone was rather mentally pre occupied with the recent turn of events, and so no one seemed to notice, or if they had, probably wouldn't care what Amelia was doing. Steve Silver was also restless, he wanted to speak to Joe in private about these new allegations, but was unable to do so while everyone was still in the room. Amelia excused herself while the lawyers and the court reporter began packing up. The room was abuzz with activity, mentally and physically.

Joe tried to scramble across the chairs to get to Amelia as she was heading out the door, "Amelia," he called, "Amelia, Amelia."

But Steve Silver grabbed him by the arm, and said earnestly, "Joe, Joe, stop! This is not the time. We'll attend to this later." Amelia looked at Joe and smiled broadly, all the while thinking, yeah Joe, I can't wait to take you back!

Andy Gold was still hysterical with laughter inside. This had quickly turned into a fiasco for Steve's client. The court reporter had a look of disdain every time she looked in Joe's direction, she had to get out of there, badly. She was the same court reporter present during Joe's deposition, and as if that wasn't bad enough.

Right after Amelia left the room there was a knock at the door.

The court reporter invited the person into the room thinking it might be someone who was a party to a deposition in the same room after them, "It's open, please come in." She really wanted to answer with, "Oh, please come in and save us!"

The door opened and a young man in a pair of jeans and a t-shirt went up to Joe. He recognized him from the picture he had been given.

"Mr. Joseph Jake Loveit?" the young man asked, ignoring the fact he was in jeans and a t-shirt and everyone else in the room was in fancy courtroom attire.

"Yes," answered Joe looking at him blankly.

"Sir, consider yourself served," said the young man, and he dumped a pile of papers into Joe's hands, and left the room.

Joe looked at his lawyer, who shrugged his shoulders. "What the fuck is this?" he yelled. A pitch no one had heard before. It was as though Joe Loveit had suddenly come alive to a bitter reality – life!

Andy Gold watched as he quietly packed up, dying with even more laughter inside. He had to get out of there too, not for the same reason as the court reporter though. He was going to burst out laughing, and he didn't feel comfortable doing it to his old time rival, Steve Silver.

"What do you mean you don't know, you're my fucking lawyer aren't you? Well, aren't you?" Joe ranted.

"Joe, you need to calm down, there are other people in the room. And yes, I am your lawyer on this case, what you have in your hands is another case, and I don't believe you have retained me for that case Joe," Steve Silver responded professionally.

"How the hell can they do this, just serve you like that at the end of a deposition. Who the hell set this shit up?" Joe bellowed.

The court reporter had quickened her pace, hurriedly packing away her court reporting machine, she didn't want any part of this one, she'd heard enough for one day. She thanked the lawyers, interrupting Joe and Steve Silver, and left.

As Andy Gold reached the door to leave he heard Steve Silver tell Joe to look at the document, and see who the petitioner was. Andy opened the door quickly, and stepped outside closing it just as quickly behind him. Standing on the other side he waited, briefcase in hand.

He heard Joe let out a huge roar. "Aaaaaaaagghhhh! That bitch! That bitch! That fucking Bitch!" And with that Andy heard a hard thump on the door behind him, he knew Joe had thrown the papers clean across the room hitting the door.

Steve Silver went to the door to pick up the papers and read the caption, well this was what Andy Gold surmised when he heard a pile of papers being shuffled behind him. After all, Steve Silver had to have been curious.

"Petitioner: Amelia Swift," Steve read aloud.

Andy Gold had heard enough. He smiled broadly. Joe Loveit's behavior had been way over the top even for him these past few months. As Andy reached the elevator, he sent a text message to Ashley: *The shit just hit the fan. All desires hoped for met, and more.* Ashley smiled and forwarded it to Amelia, and then deleted it from her inbox. Amelia smiled broadly too when she read it, and then deleted it from her inbox.

∞∞

Lily was sitting in a movie when the urgent texting began.

"Mommy, I got a txt from David. Ashley's crying. He doesn't know what 2 do."

There it is Lily thought, kids always texting you with something needing your immediate attention on your night off. But it was her daughter Ari, and Ari was one of the most responsible children she knew, so for her to text Lily like this, she knew there was an issue. Nevertheless, she also knew children panic quite easily. Moving the phone between her legs in the dark she tried to respond with the least amount of interference to others around her. Fortunately, the theatre was fairly empty.

"That's ok. Tell David crying is good 4 her," Lily responded.

Very soon after came this, "She hasn't moved for hours. In the same spot. She's stiff. She's hysterical crying. He doesn't know what 2 do. She won't listen to him. He doesn't know what 2 do," in the usual more cryptic language children use in text messages.

Then, it became apparent why the texting began in the first place, "He asked if u can come over quick. He's scared. She won't stop. U the only one she trusts. She needs u. He has no one 2 call."

There it was, Lily's calling.

Before Lily entered Ashley's house she performed her usual ritual. She said a short prayer, cleared the energies around her, and asked for assistance from the higher energies to help Ashley in a way that would serve Ashley best.

David answered the front door, his face rather ashen, a contrast to his usual pink cheeks.

"Don't worry David," said Lily, "I'm here, where's your mom?" She patted David's arm affectionately as she stepped into the house.

Almost in one breath he said, "She's in the family room, on the couch, her body is all like inflexible, hysterical, I can't get her to stop, she doesn't even hear me, she refuses to talk, she just makes that horrible sound. I called my grandma and she's all worried. She told me to call the doctor and to…but she won't move…"

As soon as David said he called his grandma, Lily knew she would need to calm that end down first. She knew only too well what it was like to be a mother, living away from her child. Her eldest daughter was away at college in New York City.

"Can you please get your Grandma on the phone for me David, while I go to your Mom?" Lily asked.

David didn't answer, he just nodded, yes. He was very afraid but also relieved an adult was finally here, and he could pass over the reigns of control.

Lily found Ashley as David described. She was howling, not just crying. She was rigid as a board sitting upright on the couch but not with her back against it. One side of her body was leaning against the sofa, the other half turned inwards to face the back of the couch, her head buried into it. Lily felt the tension as she sat down on the sofa beside her, and took her hand. It was ice cold. Lily understood all the emotional pain Ashley had locked away all these months, possibly years was manifesting in her body. She was not afraid, she never was with the power of the Universe behind her.

She spoke gently to Ashley, "It's okay Ashley, I'm here, I won't leave you, It's okay to feel all this pain, just let the pain come to the surface, everything is going to be just fine."

Ashley kept howling, while Lily lovingly rubbed Ashley's arm up and down. "I'm here, it is safe for you to cry, just let it flow, everything will get better after this."

David entered the room, his face contorting again when he heard his mother, his arm was extended holding the phone. "My grandmother," he said.

Lily got up, took the phone from David, and walked out of the room with him, her arm around his shoulder. Holding her hand over the telephone speaker Lily said calmly, "Thank you David, thank you for calling me to help. Why don't you go and check on your brother and sister, be sure they're asleep then go and watch a movie in your room. Everything is going to be fine. I'm here. I'll check in on you later." David, Lily could tell was visibly pleased to be officially released from duty. Then she placed the phone to her ear.

"Hi, this is Lily. I met you briefly when you were here over the Christmas vacation."

"Oh, I am so happy you're there Lily. What's going on, David sounded so troubled? I am so anxious here, and I am so far away. I cannot get to her. I can hear her in the background, and she refused to take the phone when I called. I just don't know what to do," Ashley's mother said, feeling at a loss on the other side.

"Please don't worry. I can handle this. I will be sure she is fine before I leave, and I will be sure David and the others are too. She seems to be overwhelmed by everything, but it's good she's releasing it now. There is a lot of emotional pain from this divorce. She will be fine, don't worry. I'm here. I will call you back a little later on." Lily reassured Ashley's mother.

"Is there anything I can do from here?" Ashley's mother asked.

"Yes, as a matter of fact there is. Pray, say a prayer for Ashley, and bless her, and ask that she be able to work through this block easily," Lily responded.

Delighted she could participate in some way Ashley's mother said, "Oh, I can do that, I do it every day. Pray for her, I mean."

"Well, that's wonderful. Do it now again, and I will call you back soon. Goodbye," Lily said, wanting to get back to Ashley.

"Goodbye, and thank you for being there with Ashley," Ashley's mother repeated.

Lily hung up, and returned to the room where Ashley was still howling.

She took Ashley's hand in hers again, and began rubbing her arm with her other hand. "Ashley, I'm here, and I won't leave you until you feel better… try to think of something wonderful in your life… it will help to balance out the pain you feeling."

Ashley blurted out, "Everything you told me is a lie! There is no God. No God is like this! This Universe kicked me in the ass! All they want to do is ruin me! All I want is peace, this life stinks…. I'm not coming back here…. I can't even be a good mother…. I hate everything…. I hate myself… he just lied…. and lied… over and over again, they just lied and lied to me all these years, everything you said was a lie…" and then she returned to her howling.

"It's okay to feel this way Ashley, it has been a painful experience all of this, having to face who you are in such a raw situation, the legal system has it's way of doing that to you, just let the pain release itself, I'm here still," Lily kept on.

"That meditation stuff is a load of shit!…. That 'be nice in the world' is a load of shit!…. That if 'you're nice, others will be nice back to you' is a load of shit!…. That 'live in the now' is a load of shit! It's all just shit, shit, shit!" Ashley shouted.

Lily was pleased. Ashley was responding nicely. She was talking again. Thank you, Lily said in her head to her Guides and Angels.

Again, she spoke to Ashley, "It's okay to feel this way Ashley, you're only human, and you have human emotions that limit you… It will pass. Try and breathe more deeply through your nose," Lily directed.

Ashley did. Her breathing regulated, and Lily could see the rhythm in Ashley's chest change.

"Now, keep breathing… deeply… deeply… and allow the peace to seep into your body…. It's right here with me…. I brought it with me… allow it to be with you… to comfort you,"

Lily said gently and quietly, and she repeated this to Ashley several times.

Ashley stopped howling. She had been at the wolf howl level for several hours. Her face red from it, her body was still unyielding, but her mind was willing to receive, Lily could tell.

Every few minutes Lily would add something to help Ashley, "Your children are sleeping peacefully, Ashley... David is calm in his room watching a movie... all is calm in your home... Just keep breathing... and make more space for that peace to enter your life line.... It so wants to soothe you."

"Leave your old life behind Ashley.... See yourself waving goodbye to it.... It no longer serves you. ...Just be peaceful... This is a peaceful and calm transition. Keep breathing.... Everything is fine," Lily continued.

Lily thought Ashley was still responding nicely. She could feel the tension in her arm begin to subside.

"It's a beautiful night outside Ashley... it's calm, and there's a wonderful soft breeze... thousands of stars and a magnificent moon... it's a new moon... a time of new beginnings... it's a fruitful time Ashley... a fulfilling time, and the night sounds, you can hear them all if you're calm and quiet..." Lily pressed.

"Keep breathing Ashley, and keep allowing the light in.... the peace... the calm, the Heavenly light....only

Heavenly light is allowed in Ashley... let it join you," Lily said in a melodic tone.

Ashley's breathing was much more even, and the stress in her arm was much less and her hand wilted within Lily's. Then Ashley began to cry, not a loud hysterical cry but a soft, intense and peaceful cry. Her tears flowed like a stream filled with the first spring rains high up in the mountains. Her crying was smooth, and mellow. It was as if she were returning to her reality in the room.

Lily kept reaffirming, "I'm here Ashley, it's ok... it's much more peaceful now around you... it's passing... just let the calm be a part of you... let the tears release the final patches of old energy... this is energy you no longer need... it's past, done with... keep breathing... deeply... evenly, let it all pass."

Ashleys hand was limp now, and the warmth had returned to it. Then the crying began to subside, and Lily could see exhaustion set in, the final release.

"You're going to feel very tired, Ashley...just let the exhaustion take over....it's a good tired...it needs to be....just let it be," Lily encouraged.

A few minutes later Lily said, "Why don't you lie down on the couch, Ashley. I'm going to cover you with this blanket here."

And so, Ashley did. She scooted down and turned her body to face the back of the couch, and Lily covered her with the blanket. As she did, Ashley's free hand reached up and took

Lily's arm. "Thank you Lily, I don't know what I would have done without you tonight. You're the only one I trust," Lily smiled, she knew it wasn't her. She thanked her guides and Angels again.

"Sleep Ashley. No one will disturb you. You will feel so much better in the morning. Much happier. Don't worry I'm going to check on the children, and I'll call your Mom too. Just sleep, let the energy move you into that safe place. I'm going to turn the light off. I'll check up on you tomorrow. Everything is just fine." Lily turned off the light and went to find David.

David was in his room with the lights off, the glow of the television lighting up one end of his room, the glow of his computer lighting up the other where he sat, on his bed. Lily called out softly to him, "David. David."

David looked up from his computer screen as soon as Lily entered his bedroom doorway. He wasn't sure what to expect, and his face showed it.

"Your Mom is fine David. She is resting on the couch, and will probably sleep there all night. Just let her sleep. Try and be sure to tell the sitter tomorrow to keep the little ones away from her. She may sleep in late, she is very tired. Please don't worry. She is going to be just fine, you'll see, like this never happened. You did the right thing tonight David. Can you get your grandma on the phone one more time for me? I know it's late but I told her I would call her back," Lily asked.

David picked up his phone, called the number and handed the phone to Lily once he heard the first ring sound. "Thank you," said Lily, and turned to leave the room.

When Ashley's mother answered Lily said, "Please don't worry everything is fine. Ashley is doing great. She is sleeping right now and my guess is she will sleep until late tomorrow. You may want to call her later in the day. I'm going to leave now," Lily said feeling quite drained herself. It was already 2:30 a.m.

"Lily, I don't know how to thank you. I am so grateful, I don't know what you did. I don't know what I would have done had you not been there," Ashley's mother said.

"Thank you. Your prayers helped a lot too. We will speak again soon. Goodbye," Lily said.

"Goodbye, and thank you so much again."

Lily stepped out into the night air. It was a beautiful warm evening. She breathed in deeply, her heart felt full.

She drove a convertible, because she loved to be in touch with nature all the time, especially when she was out and about. She would joke that it helped to neutralize all the energy of the Woodfield women running around. This time of year she kept the roof down all the time. She plopped down into the driver's seat and took in a deep breath. Her experiences always seemed to stretch her a little further each time, but nothing filled her heart more.

She sat there for a while, she didn't know for how long, she seldom looked at the clock. She put her head back, and looked up at the stars, marveling at the thought she had time and time again -- how small our lives seem when compared to the night skies. And yet, one Soul has the power to change everything. She thought of Ashley, and something came to mind: When you are down to nothing, the Universe is up to something.

Chapter TEN

Mary Weeks called to confirm the date and time of Ashley's deposition. "Don't worry, Hon.," Mary said trying to relax Ashley, "Andy said you will be the little shinning star you are. Dynamite in a small package! Is exactly what he said. Just follow everything he discussed with you, and it should be a breeze." While her words were encouraging, she wasn't the one sitting under that bright video light having her life x-rayed.

Without Lily, Ashley didn't think she could have made it thus far. Ashley's desire to visit with Lily increased daily. She only wanted to be around her, within her aura. Lily was like a magnet for her, her drug, a good drug, a comforting drug, one that never left you with a hangover or afraid of life.

Lily White lived in a less trendy subdivision of Woodfield Suburban Club, but, a rather charming one, nevertheless, as Ashley soon discovered. It was the only subdivision which was comprised of town homes, and was named Oxford Park. It sat in the center of Woodfield, and all the town homes were arranged in two concentric circles.

Ashley's friends referred to Oxford Park as the *slums* of Woodfield, even though none of them had ever driven through it, nor visited anyone who lived there. It was branded the *slums* because the market value of the homes were a good deal less than the rest of the homes in Woodfield, although all the same rules applied to it, as with any of the other subdivisions within Woodfield. The primary rule being; to live there you had to purchase a Woodfield Suburban Club membership, and there were no *slum* rates for this community. So, it remained the socioeconomically lower class, and overall fundamentally disregarded. The closest she or any of her friends ever came to entering the neighborhood was when they passed by its entrance on their way to or from the Woodfield North gate.

In Oxford Park, the inner circle of townhouses faced a lush and beautifully manicured neighborhood park. You saw the park directly in front of you as you entered. Driving the beauty of the park, and at its epicenter sat a simple set of small fountains. The fountains were blessed with the sweet tropical flavors of Gardenias, indigenous hedges to the area, four exquisitely large Royal Poinciana's, a combination of Royal and Coconut Palms, and of course a variety of seasonal Florida blossoms. Each season, all the accented flowers around Woodfield Suburban Club were changed out. It was believed, by the residents who sat on the Mother Homeowner Association board, this maintained Woodfield's appeal in the real estate market and kept it up to date.

Sometimes when the Woodfield teens were bored, or looking for a place to smoke marijuana often stolen from their parent's stash, they would gravitate to Oxford Park, and to add to the nights entertainment drop a liquid gel into the fountains, creating a fairytale sight of white foam. This, although glorious to witness upon first waking, never went down well with the Oxford Park's Homeowner Association, and the usual outpouring of do's and don't letters would flood resident's mailboxes. At that point, all neighborhood watches, which was always comprised of a group having at least one of the following characteristics in common; elderly, retired and firm believers 'there was nothing left in life to live for' would go into full alert for any unorthodox nighttime activity in the park. Upon the slightest suspicion, the security company, providing 24/7 security for Woodfield, would be summoned, and expected to lay any issue to rest, and promptly.

Although each townhouse was identical to the next, there was a rather homey and community feel about Oxford Park, and Ashley felt it from the moment she drove in. "What number did she tell you to go to, David?" Ashley asked her eldest son.

"3937, Mom I already told you," he whined, ripe with the usual preteen annoyance in his voice.

"That's okay David, you can tell me again."

"Jeeze...." David trailed off.

Ashley found the house easily, it was diagonally across from the park. She stopped and proceeded to get out of the car.

"What are you doing?" asked her son annoyed.

"Coming to see you get in okay, and to say hello to Ari's mother David," Ashley answered irritated.

"I'm a big kid now Mom, you don't have to follow me in. I can take it from here. I have my Blackberry. I'll call you when I'm ready to be picked up."

"No, David," said Ashley, "I'm coming in. I want to speak to Ari's Mom again."

"Great, another ball-your-eyes-out-again session!" David said, typical of his age.

"David, that's not nice."

"Fine. Come in then," David said, exasperated, knowing he wasn't going to win this one anyway.

Ashley smiled, and was excited to speak to Lily again. She didn't know exactly why, but she felt the familiar, strange, happy butterfly feeling in her gut. She only had these when she spoke to Lily.

They knocked on the door, which was slightly ajar. The front door sidelights were clear glass, placing the inside staircase in full view from the outside.

Ari came bouncing down the stairs, her long brown hair flowing behind her, "Oh, I have been waiting outside for you," she said addressing David.

David's face lit up, and turned red all at the same time, when he remembered his mother was still standing next to him.

Ashley smiled. "Hi, Ari," she said sweetly.

A tone that made David look back up at his mother. He was not used to this attitude from her. She sounded calm without the usual underlying hysteria. Although, she had been much calmer these past few weeks, he acknowledged.

"Hi Ashley," answered Ari.

"Mom, Ari and I are going to meet friends in Devon place (Devon Place was another subdivision within Woodfield). They're waiting for us already. See you later. I'll call when I need to be picked up," David scrambled off with Ari.

"Ari, is your Mom home?" Ashley shouted after them.

"Yeah," Ari shouted back, "She's in the courtyard. Go in."

"Thanks," said Ashley softly, but no one would have heard her anyway, the kids were well on their way already. She pressed the lock button on her remote car key, waited a split second for the noise from the car instructing her it was locked, and proceeded to enter the house.

Ashley, lightly pushed open the front door, and stepped into the foyer. The house surprised her, it was so modern. A total contrast to the traditional English cottage design, projected on the outside. The first thing she saw was a modern piece of artwork on the wall directly opposite the front door. She couldn't make heads or tails of the subject matter of the painting, it was far too elusive. She wondered why people bought works like this, let alone hang them on their walls.

"Hello," Ashley shouted from the foyer, not too loudly, but loud enough to be heard.

She looked up. The ceilings were high, and there was an open, airy feel about the whole house. On the walls going up the stairs were more art pieces, much larger than the one at the front door, but a little easier to decipher. At the top of the first flight of stairs there was another one of those "what the ????" does this one mean painting. Ashley moved further into the house.

She passed an antique two-tiered table, which must have once held sheets of music, judging by the engravings around the top. It now housed several metal hand-hammered bowls with leather wrapped strikers positioned within each. All the bowls rested on small individual cushions. They look old and battered, Ashley thought. This was Ashley's first introduction to the Tibetan singing bowl, so she would later learn. As she passed by the table she ran her finger around the rim of one of the bowls. The bowls seemed to have a magical quality about them which charmed her, and she couldn't resist touching them.

The high ceilings continued into the next room, all the walls were white, with semi-gloss white molding, but hanging everywhere were yet more massive pieces of art.

"Painting high ceilings white makes the room have a lack of cohesiveness and your home feel like an auditorium," her decorator had said defiantly, when Ashley had suggested using white. Seeing this room, Ashley knew she had been right.

This room was calming and inviting. It felt warm, and the paintings reduced the room's cavernous feel, as well as creating a fascinating energy. Some of the paintings were of real life size people, and others much more abstract. Something stirred deep inside of Ashley. She realized she wanted to keep painting. Sometimes though, her daily activities were still far too taxing to allow her the time she wanted to paint. But she knew once she left Lily today she was going to buy some more art paraphernalia. She yearned to pick up a paint brush. The light was bright. Not surprisingly though, there were good sized windows high up along the walls. The light beams seemed to split up in the room and land on every painting, literally highlighting each one individually. But there was something else.

The air smelled heavenly, a sweet, smoky floral. A scent Ashley did not know. A dreamy, warm intoxicating smell. In the center of the twelve foot rectangular wooden dinning table sat a two foot vase overflowing with tall yellow Sunflowers. Even more surprising were the two simple long wooden benches which flanked the table on either side. Pam would never have ordered two simple wooden benches on either side of her dinning room table. God forbid, without upholstery! "Waaaaay too hard for my cute little ass," she would have complained.

"Now, Ashley," she reminded herself, "Not nice energy, don't go there."

Lily's home was nothing like any of the homes Ashley had visited in Woodfield, nor was it like her own, for that matter. All the homes Ashley knew had layers of thick, lush gold fabric draped about the windows and doors, faux Italian villa accent walls, huge heavy furniture and massive pillows. And, now she thought about it, they didn't feel homey, just overdone. When it became fashionable for the drapes to be longer than the windows, everyone she knew reordered thick taffeta drapes which would puddle on the floor and look as if the owner had loads of money to just lie around the floors.

But the colors were all the same, various shades of beiges, golds, and creams. Bright colors were taboo, pastels outdated, and sparsely or Japanese styled furniture too low for high ceilings, cold and empty. The first wall you saw in this home as you entered the foyer, was bright fire-engine red. And, there were no drapes either, just sleek white modern sliding shades, which were drawn back revealing an enchantingly captivating courtyard.

The courtyard was in full view off the living room. Four eight foot high glass sliding doors separated it from the inside. One of the doors were open.

"Oh, Hi Ashley, please come and join me," said Lily from the courtyard. "I do hope you're not allergic to incense. Some people seem to be, but I burn it all the time."

"No, no," said Ashley being awakened from her trance. "No, it smells nice. I have never burned incense before."

"Well, you should. It clears all the dead heavy energy around your home."

"It's nice to see you again Ashley."

"Thank you, it's nice to see you again, too, Lily."

"I'm brewing a pot of passion tea. Would you like some iced? It really is deliciously fresh on hot days like these."

"Sure," said Ashley having no idea what passion tea tasted like.

"I love your courtyard," Ashley said stepping outside.

"Oh, this is not just a courtyard Ashley, this is my faerie garden."

That's it! That is exactly what it looked like! One of those faerie gardens you saw in Madison's storybooks, and it felt different to any other courtyard Ashley had ever been in. Lily's words led Ashley to notice miniature glass bowls of faerie dust strategically placed in and around the courtyard. The sun catching the sparkle here, and there eliciting rainbow beams of light. Flowers in rich bloom bounced off from everywhere.

Lily looked like a blossom in her deep indigo dress. The light cotton clung to her petite body, and dropped loosely around her feet. Ten dainty toes peeked from beneath the dress, revealing decorated toenails in a lighter shade of lavender. On her two big toes were minuscule drawings of white clouds. Lily had a full head of deep burgundy hair, green eyes, and dangling from her neck a rather large quartz crystal fashioned to a point at one end.

Tucked away in the one corner of the courtyard was a two foot fountain, a fairy sitting on the edge of an embankment holding a lily, out of which trickled water. Varieties of orchids twisted around a twelve foot palm, while a thick vine wrapped itself around another, swathed in dozens of small orange flowers. White and yellow lilies grew on the periphery of the fountain. In the background released from a small hidden speaker were beautifully soft Gregorian chants. Ashley suddenly felt very tired and wanted to curl up on the lounge chair and fall asleep in this magical peaceful haven.

"I see the pressures of life are weighing you down Ashley," Lily said observantly.

"How can you always tell when there is something wrong with me?" asked Ashley.

"Oh, there is nothing wrong with you Ashley," answered Lily as she entered her home through another set of sliding doors, this one leading into her kitchen, "You just need to learn how to relax and escape from the stresses of life."

"Why don't you sit in one of those chairs in the shade, take off those shoes of yours," Lily flapped her right hand back and forth as if irritated Ashley was even wearing shoes, "and put your feet on the Earth. I will be right out with those passion teas."

How odd. Ashley would never be told this if she had entered Pam's house. Pam would have grabbed her at the door, shooed the kids off to play, and pulled her into her bedroom, at the same time yelling for the housekeeper to deliver two cups of coffee to them as soon as possible. She would then shut the door to her bedroom, and begin an intensely action packed half hour monologue which always included who was sleeping with who's husband and/or wife in Cheshire, a critique of her neighbors latest fashion sense, and other senseless repartee.

When the children wandered in uninvited, crying or sniffing with colds, she would quickly call in the housekeeper to keep them occupied while she had a guest. The housekeeper, a foreign middle aged female, would begrudgingly take the children out of the room, complain the kitchen was short of some kind of food item or another, and then glumly inform her she was leaving early that day because she had to pick up her own child from school.

Pam would have invariably forgotten the need for her to leave early, and then instruct her to call the sitter to come in earlier, and to be sure the sitter could stay till later because she was going to the Woodfield Club House for dinner that evening.   Once the housekeeper left the room Pam would turn to Ashley and make some personal comment about how miserable the woman always was and dressed, and return to her relentless blathering.

Ashley followed Lily's instructions. She first placed her bunch of keys with the "Yes, It hurts looking this GOOD" tag hanging from them, down on the table. She left her purse in the car on the floor on the passenger side, but the car was locked, and besides it's Woodfield. She wore a pair of black Juicy couture drawstring terry pants and a sugar lips black top. She had ordered the pants online from Saks, one day when Amber was over, and they were bored and decided to browse the websites of all the shops in the mall. Where she had bought her top she couldn't recall. It was one of the oldest pieces of clothing in her wardrobe, at least 2 years old, but she had a special love for it, and just couldn't bring herself to part with it, even though she had subsequently bought three other black tops very similar to it, to replace this one.

The ground felt good beneath Ashley's feet. Hmm, she thought, when did I last do this? Come to think of it, when did I ever do this?

On a wooden table alongside her sat two large frosted bowls. More bowls, she thought. But unlike the other bowls each of these sat on a small wooden box. Next to the bowls was a strange looking instrument. It was a wooden stick about eight inches long with a small round rubber ball at its base.

"What are these for?" Ashley asked Lily when she returned, carrying two rosy pink drinks jingling with ice.

"Oh, those are music bowls. We are having a meditation circle tonight. It's a full moon. Full moons are a time to purge all your negative energies. You know you should join us. I bet you haven't been to one of these before, they are wonderfully relaxing and help center you. Why don't you come?" Lily said enthusiastically.

Oh, my G…, Ashley thought what would the women of Cheshire think if they saw me dancing under the moon light next to one of the Woodfield lakes to the sounds of frosted glass music bowls? She smiled inside.

"You know Lily, I think I will come. What time is it?" Lily gave Ashley all the details, and then she sat down to drink her passion tea.

The two chatted about abstract spiritual concepts, past lives, love, God. Concepts Ashley said she had once discussed with her grandmother, who she had a special soft spot for, and still had even after her death, all these years later.

"Your grandmother is telling me," said Lily out of the blue, "that you need to go back to the time when you had that toy horse under the tree. She wants you to remember how you felt then. She also said she loves the fountains in the park," Lily waited, "Does any of this mean anything to you Ashley, because it doesn't have meaning for me? I just get the messages. I don't try to interpret them."

Ashley thought for a moment, "Oh, yes of course they do!" she exclaimed as she remembered.

"Well, first of all," Ashley said, "she loved fountains, and I have a picture in my photo album of her standing in front of her favorite one in Spain. The toy she is referring to was a time in my life where I was creative, content, and very inquisitive. We would sit for hours under a beautiful huge old tree in her front garden, chatting about the world and what we wanted to see happen in it. All the while I twirled that little toy horse around and around in my fingers. Nice things, you know? Peaceful. Good things. Things we could do to help the Earth..." She trailed off into a blissful daze.

"That sounds really special," Lily remarked. Ashley just smiled.

"Our path does not cross with other peoples paths randomly Ashley, they are designed this way. I was meant to give you that message from your grandmother," Lily added.

"Oh, Lily you have given me a lot more than you can ever imagine. I've begun to feel happy again. I enjoy being with my children so much more, and I don't feel so rushed anymore. I have a lot to do still, but I do everything much more slowly. And when Joe calls, it doesn't irritate me as much, and I never thought I would see that day!" Ashley giggled.

"Thank you, Ashley. I'm just pleased you are receptive," Lily said, thinking back on how many clients would ask deep soul searching questions of her, but upon receiving the answers refusing to acknowledge them, and ultimately doing the exact opposite to what they had been informed, causing an untold amount of further pain and misery for themselves.

But it was not for Lily to reprimand them, she had done her part. She had imparted the messages, the rest was up to the person who received them. It was their free will to either acknowledge the information or reject it. But Lily understood. Sometimes it was very challenging to accept guidance which ran contrary to social pressures, even when those social pressures had been unconsciously contrived by you.

Ashley laughed to herself over how all her friends would react if they could only see and hear what she was talking about now. She felt she could share almost anything with Lily. Lily had a way of looking at you, in the eye, shutting down the world and all of its pressures as if it had stopped, and the only things left in it was you and her. It is amazing how clear your thinking can become when the world shuts down.

Ashley began to tell Lily about the girl in high school who had warned her about Joe, and about Pam, how she suspected Pam had slept with Joe all those years ago, and then she told Lily about her blue shoes, the ones she just knew Brianna had stolen from her. She rambled on and on.

Eventually, Lily turned to her and said, "You know Ashley, you are carrying a lot of baggage around with you. Every time you encounter a new drama in your life you pull the back pack off your back, search around inside it and pull out what 'you' think is a similar incident from your past, and then you react to it in the same emotional way as before, kind of like re-enacting the same old, same old."

"Then you tangle yourself up. You see because every time you encounter an issue with someone you also connect an invisible cord to this person, and you carry that cord around with you entangling yourself, and therefore never being able to release yourself from that person. You create this network of invisible cords, like the vine over there. Aren't you just tired of all of this?" she questioned.

"You are preventing yourself from moving forward, Ashley. In fact, you can't move forward, because you're still attached to people and events in your life which happened years ago. And, rather than experiencing a new moment with new elements when you meet someone, you are squashing all the possible goodness that experience may possess to pass onto you because of past gobble-de-goop. You have to learn to forgive," Lily said trying to enlighten Ashley.

"But I can't forgive them, it's like me telling them they've won," Ashley said shocked.

"No," said Lily, "it is not like that at all. Because if you forgive someone Ashley, it does not mean you have to agree with what they have said, or done or what they stand for, it is a way of releasing yourself and them from holding you back. It's a way to peacefully release yourself, so you can close the door to never return to that particular issue or moment in your life ever again. It's the past Ashley, can't change the past it's complete, all you can do is work in the now as I told you before," Lily explained.

"Look, why don't you do this exercise I once read about. It was suggested by a wonderful spiritual soul. It will be very beneficial to you," Lily suggested.

"Go to the ocean when you have some quiet time. You will probably need a few hours. Go by yourself. Take a paper and pen with you. Find a calm spot away from everyone, and then begin to make a list of everyone who has ever hurt you, upset you, or just annoyed you. And don't forget to add in pets or other animals. Any living creature who and whom has caused you frustration. As you write each name down place a big imaginative 'X' sign through their name," Lily animated this by making a big 'X' into the air to emphasize her point.

"Then," she continued, "tell them you release them, you forgive them, you release yourself and you forgive yourself, and then release them in a balloon into the atmosphere to go up and away forever."

"You will find, Ashley, after this release you will feel lighter, and even more free than you feel right now. It's time Ashley. It's time to let the past go. It's done. Don't drag this awful dead energy around. You cannot create the life of your dreams for yourself and your family if you don't close the doors to the past," Lily ended.

"I understand what you mean," Ashley said, "I just had no idea how preoccupied I was with my past until you pointed it out to me. And I do want a fresh start, I truly do."

At that moment an idea popped into Ashley's head. I'll tell Lily afterwards, she thought.

∞∞

Ashley had never been to a meditation circle before, let alone a full moon meditation circle. They all met at someone's home, no-one Ashley had ever met before, but the house strangely enough was on the water not too far from Joe's mother's house. This tickled Ashley, if she could only see me now, she thought of Marjorie.

There were nine of them. Nine being the number of completion and reward in numerology, Ashley was later enlightened by the host. They all took a mat and lay flat on their backs. Ashley placed her mat next to Lily's. The moon appeared brilliant, bright, and plump.

The host asked everyone to close their eyes and clear their minds. Ashley did her best, clearing one's mind, so she had discovered since learning to meditate these past few months was a challenge for any human being. The host helped her by saying, "and for all those first timers here tonight, just try and let your mind loose, to wander, don't try and control it. Best if you can think of something you love, like a flower, or a tree and try to focus on that."

Then the host began to explain how he was going to create music with the set of music bowls which were laid out in a half moon shape before him. Ashley had seen the spread of music bowls when she arrived. They appeared to be a set, but some were the same size, others not. There was even a heart shaped bowl in the center. It was the only one which wasn't frosted glass.

"Each one," continued the host, "has a different note, but when played together their sounds will blend melodically. All the sounds from the bowls are balanced with one another, as you will soon hear."

With that the meditation began. The host was skillful, and had every part of Ashley's body relaxed, including her mind within minutes. Ashley being so stressed from life and her impending deposition, hadn't realize it made her a prime candidate for relaxation. Like a tuning fork she was infused into the melody of the singing bowls, all thoughts and the outside world washed away. She could no longer feel any part of her body. The air felt light, and she became unaware of anyone else being present except for her and the singing bowls.

The bowls were exquisitely beautiful, like nothing she had ever heard in her entire life. She forgot she was Ashley, or a mother of three, or that she was going through a divorce, selling her home, or anything. Everything lost its hold on her completely. She was in a place she never wanted to leave.

After a while the host sensing his group had reached very high levels of relaxation gently began to bring them all back to the present, all the while using the bowls magical voices to reconnect each of their Earthly strings to place them where they lay in the meditation circle.

When Ashley was finally instructed to open her eyes she felt like she had been away for hours, although the entire meditation start to finish was a total of forty minutes. As she raised the top half of her body up, and sat on her mat she felt relaxed, no more pain in her lower back, no more pain in her hips, no more pain anywhere. Most of all, Ashley was for the first time in her life since a child, present, right here in the very moment. She felt it. Her breathing was even. She knew this was the *now* Lily had spoken about.

While they sat around a small wooden table afterwards, still outside next to the water, eating from small ceramic bowls filled with a scrumptious hearty soup (the host believing it would ground them before they left), they each shared their feelings from the meditation. Some had gone to distant lands, or so it sounded to Ashley, some had experienced visions of color, and yet others conversations with Angels. When it came to Ashley's turn she felt a little intimidated, but also overwhelmed.

"All I felt was peace, a glorious peace, I have not felt my whole life, that I can ever remember," she said, streams of tears flowing from her eyes.

Lily smiled. Ashley had landed on soft ground and the rebuilding had begun.

Chapter ELEVEN

Woodfield Suburban Clubhouse was a hot spot for children's parties, especially between the ages of five and ten. Vendors would swarm the lawns overlooking its massive manmade lake early on a Saturday morning to pump air into their thirty and forty foot bounce houses, and assorted waterslides. The waterslides were often a combination of the Hurricane, the Tornado, the Pipeline, and the Tsunami waterslides, all promising a different kind of water saturation experience for your children.

There was always one blow up game for the older kids, usually an interactive sports unit, the most popular being a water balloon war station. With this feature there was a water balloon filling station, and two battle stations, one opposite the other, both protected by netting. Teams would be chosen, and each team got to occupy a battle station. Balloons would be filled, then launched from balloon launchers. As each water balloon hit the opponents net it would explode drenching everyone behind it. For all those kids subjected to private school rules and regulations each week, this was a great release.

A Marquee was often set up alongside the play areas providing a sanctuary for parents, and nannies, where they could chat and keep out of the sun and the constant flow of water. Along the lakeside embankment there would be a row of food stations, anything from barbeques to Italian fast food, and ice-cream stands. From the main street of Woodfield encircling the Woodfield Suburban Clubhouse these birthday parties looked like organized fairs and festivals, and for any uninvited child, a reason to stop, and stare with envy.

Pam found a parking, hustled her children out of the car, and casually made her way over to the marquee, her arms overflowing with the birthday child's gifts, her children charging ahead too excited to stay within her slow pace. She wore a light cotton sun dress from a trendy Barcelona store, a cute Juicy cap, a pair of Michael Kors sunglasses, and because she was going to be on the grounds, and didn't want her skinny heels to catch the fresh dirt, she chose a pair of beige wedges. Her simple, four carat diamond choker necklace sparkling as she walked. The necklace was a gift to herself, once her divorce from John became final – "for all the pain and suffering you caused me John," she said to herself smiling, as she majestically placed it around her neck for the first time. Her next diamond, she thought to herself, would be an engagement ring, one from a *real* man, nothing like John, but the man of her dreams.

Amber, Brianna, and Taylor were already there, their children well into the mix, with nannies out in the field watching. For the Woodfield women tuning out to the sounds of screaming and shouting was their forte. A children's party like this one was like a private girl's coffee date.

"It's just impossible to get out of our house on time these days," said Pam exasperated, as she approached her friends, who were comfortably seated in the Marquee, sipping their individually prepared Starbucks drinks. Although, there was often ample food and drinks at these parties catered to the adults, it was seldom touched by them. Until such time as the hosts began serving *Red Bull's*, or any other artificially spiked metabolic booster drink, these parents would continue to arrive with their personally prepared drinks, and nurse them over the two or three hour duration of the party.

This day, Pam did not have time to pick up her own drink, so she called Taylor to pick one up for her. Taylor was more than happy to accommodate Pam's request, and made sure the Barista prepared Pam's order to a 'T,' just as her text message had read.

Pam finally sat down after dropping the birthday gift off on the 'gift' table, and began a conversation. Taylor passed her, her drink.

"Thanks, Tay."

Then changing the subject, "Any of you seen Ashley lately?" she asked.

Everyone looked at one another and shook their heads.

"I really don't know what's up with her these days. I call her and then she doesn't call back for a day or so, and then when she does call me back she can't talk because she has some meeting or other to attend," Pam said in a judgmental tone.

"Why does she bother to call me at that time then at all?" she continued to find fault. "Do you think that she and Joe are having problems?" she said, prying for information.

Brianna chipped in, "Well, I don't know her or Joe too well. I only met them that one time. I have been meaning to get their number from Amber and call her for months but every time I think I have some free time to call and make plans with them, something comes up. But I haven't seen her anywhere, not even in Cheshire." If Brianna had been totally honest she would have said, "but then again people seldom saw their neighbors in Cheshire. If you saw a neighbor it was usually at Starbucks, some deli, or a restaurant where you would run into them."

But she didn't, rather she continued to add to the pot, "But even that one time I met her, she left *Aqua* without even saying good-bye, and Michael and I talked about it afterwards, we couldn't work it out, eventually we thought it must have been sitter issues, but maybe it wasn't, maybe it was more."

"Hey, there's Nina with the children, maybe we should try and see what we can get out of her," Amber said, inside squirming with delight as she took the lead in what she believed was an investigative mission. With that, Amber furiously waived Nina to come over.

"Hi, Nina," Amber said sweetly. The usual sweet greeting Nina knew only too well.

Here it comes, Nina thought, the meddling. It is almost too much for them to resist.

"How's everything Nina?" Amber asked.

One thing Nina liked about this set up in Woodfield was the fact that all these woman had employees who were in a constant state of misery, they all hated their jobs, and employers, but knew their services were in such high demand, curt responses to any and all questions carried little to no consequences. Their employers always reacting in the same way to their curtness; they just ignored it. Mainly, because for them they tolerated whatever it took to have their time to go to the gym, the mall, the hair and nail salon, and any other activity they had secretly going on.

"They had skin like crocodiles!" Nina would say, no attitude would topple them. If she was an employer she would never have put up with half of it. But sometimes these habits paid off, especially during times like these.

Nina chose to aggravate them even more by answering with a single word, "Fine."

But as usual the women were persistent, "Ashley and Joe okay?" Amber asked, and before Nina could respond, Amber quickly followed up with, "I haven't seen them in ages and I well...we were wondering if they were doing okay?" She was trying to be discreet, but Nina knew exactly what she was up to, her usual, no good gossip.

"They're fine," Nina responded, and turned her back to the woman, her lips unlocking a massive smile as she pretended to look out into the sea of children.

Addressing Nina's back Amber said, "Matthew came home from school the other day and said Joe, Jr told him his father was buying a new house outside of Woodfield. Do you know about this Nina?" The other three women turned to look at Amber in shock, all six pairs of eyebrows raised simultaneously.

Pam mouthed the words to Amber without sound, "He did!"

"Nope," said Nina without turning back around, "First I've heard of it."

"Well, don't you think you should find out, Nina? I mean you could *lose* your job?" Amber said, this time trying to *really* push the envelope.

Madison saved the day for Nina. At the far end of the tract of grass, she started crying, and running around in circles calling out Nina's name.

Nina, spotted her and said, "I have to go, Amber's crying." With that she sprinted off towards Amber.

Once Nina left, Pam turned to Amber, "You didn't tell me that! Why didn't you call and tell me? You know Ashley is my best friend. Why didn't you call and tell me what Matthew said?"

"Well, he only told me yesterday Pam, and it's not like it's the hottest news in town," Amber answered sarcastically.

"Yes, but it is 'Ashley,' Amber, not some stranger," emphasized Pam. Brianna, and Taylor were quiet.

"Well, so what if Joe's buying a new house?" Amber said deflated. She had begun a perfectly well organized line of investigative questioning with Nina to help Pam, and all the thanks she received was a slap in the face.

"What the Fuck!" Pam raised her voice, "Of course it matters. Don't you see? Maybe Joe was part of that New York 'Maddoff' scheme, you know the guy who 'made off' with everyone's money, and may be he lost all his money and now they have to sell their house and live in some cheap neighborhood! Maybe Joe, Jr. overheard Joe and Ashley talking about Joe going out to buy a new house. That matters Amber! Ashley could be having to sell all her jewelry and clothes to make ends meet and too embarrassed to face us all. Oh, what a fool I've been. My best friend has lost everything, loosing her home, all her children's college funds, and here I am not even supporting her. I'm going to call her today, right after this party. I feel so guilty. What kind of a best friend am I?" Pam questioned herself after her resolution.

"Maybe you should take it a little slower Pam," said Taylor trying to be useful, "I mean, I wouldn't go off and tell her what Matthew said, rather just wait for her to tell you. I mean, it's like you said, maybe she's too embarrassed and that's why she didn't tell us in the first place. I mean, poor Ash."

"Yeah," I agree with Taylor, said Brianna, "and to think Michael and Joe were going to be business partners. Maybe, I should speak to Michael and see if he can arrange some kind of a deal to help Joe earn some money. Oh, this is so tragic. What a terrible thing to happen to such a nice couple. This must be the reason why they left *Aqua* so quickly that night, maybe Joe got some bad news, I saw him checking his e-mail when we got the second round of drinks. No, maybe he was checking his bank account! Oh, how awful, maybe they didn't have enough money to pay for that round of drinks we ordered. This is all too awful for words," Brianna added to the growing drama.

Pam's phone rang, she checked the caller I.D. before answering. Excitedly with her hand she gestured to her friends to keep their voices down, she ever so quietly announced it was Ashley calling.

"Just be calm, like nothing's happened, let Ashley tell us herself," Brianna repeated in a whisper.

"Hi Ash," answered Pam warmly. The groups eyes affixed on her.

"Hi, Pam," responded Ashley even more warmly.

"Pam, do you have some time this afternoon to meet with me?" Ashley asked.

"She wants to meet," Pam mouthed the words to the others, holding her first two fingers over the speaker, just in case she was overheard.

On the other end, Ashley was smiling, she could just imagine the scene -- Pam covering the speaker with her fingers relaying to the others what Ashley was saying on the phone. Ashley had attended so many of those birthday parties, after all David was a preteen already.

"Of course Ash, what time did you have in mind?" Pam acting like the faithful friend she believed she was.

"Oh... how's about two o'clock?" Ashley responded.

"Sounds good. Do you want to come to my house?" Pam asked.

"That sounds fine," Ashley said, "See you later, and enjoy the party Pam."

Before Pam could say thanks, Ashley had cut the call.

"That is so strange," Pam said, "Ashley just cutting me off like that, she must be sooooo distressed."

"Now, Pam, you just need to be calm and let her tell you everything. All you can do is be there for her. You cannot make anything right. In times like these all we can do is be there for one another, isn't that right girls?" Amber rambled on with instructions, Taylor and Brianna nodding their heads in agreement.

Ashley in the meantime was preparing for her visit to Pam. She lit a few sticks of incense, and began an hour-long guided meditation to relax herself completely. She wanted to be very calm and centered when she spoke to Pam today. She went to her Angel Oracle Cards, energetically cleared the deck by asking Archangel Michael to clear the energy, and then she pulled a few cards asking the Angels to give her some guidance for the day. She pulled the card "Stand your ground," and "You and your loved ones are protected," and finally, the one which read, "Take a leap of faith." With that Ashley felt confident she was doing exactly what was needed of her. She completed her ritual with a personal prayer to God for mother Earth, and for all the Souls she would encounter that day.

At exactly two p.m. Ashley rang Pam's doorbell. Pam came leaping down the stairs as if she were a teen about to meet her date, hollering out to her housekeeper she would get the door, and she would like two coffee's up in her room. Ashley heard Pam's coffee request, and smiled.

Ashley, dressed all in white, was glowing, and Pam was taken aback when she opened the door. This was not the picture Pam was expecting. Certainly not how someone down and out should look. But maybe she is just really good at covering it up, Pam assumed. Pam was a master at working the picture to fit her judgments.

"Hi," said Ashley with a beautiful broad smile. She was positively gorgeous Pam thought.

"Hi Ash," Pam said leaning her head to one side, in her kindest tone, like she was visiting someone sick in the hospital, "please come in, I'm all yours." And she proceeded to pull Ashley into the house.

"What is that smell you have on Ash? I don't know it," Pam asked kindly.

"Lavender," answered Ashley.

"Oh," said Pam puzzled. She was used to Ashley's usual Channel.

When they got into Pam's bedroom, Pam closed the door behind them. She then got onto her bed and patting the bed beside her told Ashley to join her. Just like in high school, Ashley reminded herself. But Ashley didn't sit on the bed beside Pam she remained standing by the side of it.

"Pam," Ashley began, "I have something to ask you, and I would ask that you please not lie to me and tell me the truth. It's very important to me that you tell me the exact and honest truth."

Pam began to feel a little uneasy but tried to appear interested in what Ashley was about to say.

"That day in high school, the day I met you outside the boys locker room when you said you were there to find the binder you had loaned to Rob, did you have sex with Joe?"

Pam's mouth went dry. What the hell was this? She thought, Oh my G… this was years ago!

"Pam," Ashley urged, "*Please*, I need to know the truth. Did you sleep with my boyfriend?"

"Ash," said Pam, "I don't know what to say to that. I mean you're talking about high school, a billion years ago."

"I know," said Ashley, "but I need to know… now."

"How many times, Pam, did you have sex with Joe behind my back? If we are going to have any kind of friendship after this Pam I need to know the truth," Ashley said calmly but firmly, so calm in fact, she seemed to surprise herself.

In a very soft pitch, Pam said, "Three times. We had sex three times. I'm really, really sorry Ash. I just didn't know how to tell you. I wanted to after the first time, and then you know what it's like, you young and your hormones are raging and Joe was so ..." Pam faded and began to twist her shirt around and around her fingers.

"Convincing?" Ashley softly finished Pam's sentence, "Yes, I know. Thank you Pam," Ashley said gently, "Thank you for telling me the truth. You see, I always had a feeling, I just couldn't be sure, and I didn't have the confidence to hear what you would say, until now. I don't hate you Pam. It was a very long time ago. I'm here to forgive you Pam, truly forgive you. I need to release you and myself from this pain. Please understand that. It is time for me to let go of this past, and for you, too."

Pam followed part of what Ashley was saying but the 'release you and myself,' part she just couldn't understand. Her thoughts were interrupted as the housekeeper knocked at the door with the coffees.

"Please leave it outside," said Ashley taking charge, and realizing she had shocked Pam into speechlessness. This was a first! She thought.

This conversation, Ashley guessed, was the one conversation Pam after all these years would never have guessed would ever come her way.

"I'm moving on Pam. I'm divorcing Joe. I should have done this a long time ago. Well, no, actually let me correct that.

This is the perfect time. The time has finally come for me to say goodbye to Joe. Don't be sad for me. I'll be just fine. Please remember I don't hate you, and I forgive you. Thank you for seeing me. I have to go now," Ashley opened the door to Pam's bedroom to let herself out. Pam, still sitting on the bed speechless, didn't look up. She felt as if she'd been stabbed through the heart.

At the door Ashley stepped over the tray holding the coffee cups the housekeeper had left outside the room. After leaving Pam, Ashley did what Lily had taught her, she moved her hands up and down in front of her cutting the imaginary cords which connected her to Pam. She lifted her hand over her head and reaching as far back as she could, without falling down the stairs, she imitated cutting cords down her back also. The cords between her and Pam were thoroughly disengaged. This she said to herself, is my release, I forgive myself. I will no longer think of this ever again.

Walking to her car Ashley called Amber. "Hi, Amber," she said.

"Oh, Hi Ash, how are you?" Amber asked.

"Fine," Ashley said meaning it. Amber thought how close her answer sounded to Nina's earlier that day.

"Do you have Brianna's cell number by any chance?" Ashley asked.

Amber was hot on the trail. She remembered the conversation at the party earlier in the day. Brianna may be able to help. Oh, she wouldn't hesitate to give Ashley Brianna's number.

"Of course Ash, here it is…" Brianna gave her the number and waited.

"Thanks," said Ashley.

"Hey, Ash if there's anything I can help you with, I mean *anything* please call me," Amber said before saying goodbye.

"Sure, thanks," responded Ashley, knowing if she ever needed anything Amber would probably be the last person on her list she would call.

Ashley dialed Brianna's number. "Hi, Brianna, it's Ashley, remember you met me at *Aqua* with Amber?"

Brianna was taken by surprise. How did Ashley get my number? And why was she calling me out of the blue like this? They had just spoken about her today? She hadn't even had a chance to speak to Michael yet. How surreal this all felt.

"Brianna, I know this may seem strange but I need to see you about something. Can you find a half an hour to see me today?" Ashley asked.

At first, Brianna wanted to say no, but her curiosity got the better of her, "Well, the sitter will be here at three, I could meet with you a little after that, if you like?"

"Perfect," said Ashley, "I know you live right behind me. I will see you around four fifteen. That way you can get the kids settled in with the sitter first."

Ashley called Joe, "Hi, Joe," she said.

"Ash, is this going to take long?" he responded.

"Well, I do need about five minutes of your time. Do you have that right now for me?" she said, "It's important."

"Ash, if this is about the lawyers, and ...well, you really need to get your lawyer to call mine on Monday morning..." He snapped.

"No," said Ashley interrupting him, "it has nothing to do with the divorce."

"Okay, give me five and call me back," he agreed.

"Fine, five minutes." Five minutes later Ashley called Joe back.

"Joe," she said, "I know about you and Pam having sex in high school, and I know now you lied to me about a lot of girls and women you slept with, and well I just want to tell you I forgive you, and I release you, and I release myself." There was silence on the other end of the phone.

Ignoring the silence, Ashley continued, "I want to be done with you and the past Joe. I don't care how many women you betrayed me with Joe, while we were married, but its over, and I'm happy it is, and if you want to have primary control of the children you can, Joe. I feel comfortable in my decisions, and I want you to also. And tell your Mother I forgive her also, and I release her, and it is ok, I know she loves you, and just wanted the best for you," Ashley said clearly without stopping.

"Woah, Woah, Woah, hold it there Ash, are you feeling okay? Have you been drinking, taking any meds?" Joe said, his usual suspicious nature shinning through, "What's all this release stuff?"

"No, Joe, I'm perfectly fine. I have no fight with you. I accept we're done, and I don't have anything against what's her name? Mel. I hope you will be happy together. I forgive Mel, and I release her too," Ashley continued, and then was silent.

"Joe, are you still there?" Ashley asked, a huge smile spread across her face. One, Joe could not see. This forgiveness thing was beginning to feel really, really good to her.

"Yes, I'm here Ash. I'm sorry, too, Ash. I never meant to hurt you. I guess we were just too young for all of this. My mother has been really intense about this divorce, and you were right she has it out for you. I just don't think she ever really liked you Ash, and you know I don't know what it is. But I'm sorry, Ash. You know, I don't want to take the kids. She was just trying to get back at you. I will tell my lawyer on Monday to drop it. This is a good thing you did Ash, it's time to wrap this all up. I am moving to New York City, but I guess you figured that one out too?" Joe said, sounding unusually sincere, -- as sincere as Joe could be, Ashley thought.

Of course he would never want to be the primary parent for the children, she knew that, far too restricting on Joe's freedom. Watch out Mel! Or maybe Mel will be Joe's match, she thought, then shrugged disinterested in the outcome. Your journey Joe, not mine. Center Ash, she instructed herself, keep your thoughts kind.

"The agent called me an hour ago, did he get hold of you?" Joe asked.

"No, but there is a message in my voice mail, I haven't yet listened to," Ashley responded.

"He has an offer on the house, I think we should take it. I'll pay for a rental in the neighborhood for you and the kids until David and Joe, Jr. finish the school year, and then you can look for a new place," Joe said.

Wow, Ashley thought, if only I had tried these magic words on him before! She had forgotten, in all her painful victimhood daze Joe always had to have a woman take the lead, he seldom took any initiative, except when it came to sex.

"What's the offer Joe?" she asked.

"Well, put it this way we won't make any money, but we won't loose any either," He said.

Ashley thought about it for a moment. She wouldn't want any money from the house anyway, it would be tainted. Tainted with pain and anguish she didn't need or want, she wanted a fresh start.

"Call him and tell him we'll take it then," Ashley said.

That was the moment Ashley was done with Joe. Finally, she cut Joe loose from her life, and now she could get on with hers, and Joe with his.

∞∞

Joe, on the other hand, was still overwhelmed by the turn of events, and so called his mother.

"Mom, I just had the strangest call from Ashley. She said she forgives me and forgives you and understands you were just doing the best for me, and she knows how important I am to the children and *how much I have done for them*." Typical Joe, he just couldn't help himself kicking in the last part of the sentence.

But Joe's wheels were always turning, he needed his mother to give up this fight also, and it just seemed like the only way at that moment.

"She really sounded sincere, Mom. I'm going to drop the fight for primary caretaker of the children on Monday. I want this all over and behind me, after all I don't want two cases at once, I still have Amelia to deal with. I really want to move to New York now. I can handle my case with Amelia from there."

"Well, I'm glad she finally came to her senses. That girl always had an issue with me. She really needed to start to see the wood for the trees. I'm so glad you're done with her. We certainly showed her. Maybe she went to therapy or something, even her therapist probably told her to give up the fight. She really acted stupidly this time," Marjorie Patterson said in her usual deluded way, and completely contaminated with hate.

Even Joe felt agitated from her comment. It's really time to leave, he thought.

"What did you want for dinner tonight, Joe? I was thinking of ordering in Chinese…" Marjorie changed the subject.

∞∞

Before Ashley was scheduled to see Brianna she had some time to kill. There was something else she needed to do.

She went to her computer and logged onto Facebook. Now what was the girl's name again from school, the one who warned me about Joe, the one I ranted off to Pam about? Ashley tried to search back into her memory. Of course, she said to herself, Josselyn, Josselyn Wright. Ashley searched for a Josselyn Wright. What if she is married and doesn't have the same name anymore? Well at least I would have tried, that accounts for something, she placated herself. Then she saw it, Josselyn Wright. She sent off a request to Josselyn to be her friend on Facebook. She would just have to wait for her response.

Ashley arrived on Brianna's doorstep at 4:15 on the nose. Brianna answered the door.

"Hi Ashley, how are you?" she said, a little apprehensive.

"Fine, thanks Brianna," Ashley responded, "Is there somewhere private we can talk?"

"Yes, Michael's den. He's at the gym," she answered.

"Perfect," Ashley said.

Brianna was still puzzled by Ashley's sudden phone call and visit. They both entered the den, after passing her two young sons in the playroom, romping around with the sitter.

"What's this about?" Brianna asked getting straight to the point with a smidgen of irritation. Brianna wasn't one for surprises.

In a calm and clear voice Ashley got straight to the point, "Brianna when I first met you at *Aqua* you were wearing a pair of blue shoes. Where did you get those blue shoes?" Ashley had learned a lot since her first meeting with Marge.

Brianna's heart fell, into her stomach. What's this got to do with 'Maddoff,' and Ashley losing her house? She thought.

"What do you mean?" Brianna answered Ashley's question with a question, her face, she could feel, becoming very warm.

"Well….simply, where did you get the shoes?" Ashley asked again.

"I ordered them online," Brianna said, her tone much lower. Brianna was well versed in fashion, she watched all the fashion shows on television, the ones she missed she would catch up later on YouTube. She knew there was no local store between here and Miami which would stock those shoes.

"Brianna, I'm going to ask you a question, and I would truly appreciate it, if you would be totally honest with me. I am not here to judge you, I just really need to know the truth," Ashley continued.

"Did you really order those shoes on line, or did the Fedex guy just leave them on your doorstep by mistake?" Ashley asked directly.

But before Brianna could say anything Ashley continued, "You see Brianna, I ordered and paid for those very same blue Gucci shoes on line a week earlier. But the funny thing is they didn't arrive. I ordered them to wear the 'very same' Saturday night I met you! You know it took me ages to work out what happened, and I only just saw it when I was rummaging for some paperwork for my lawyer. I literally stumbled upon the on-line confirmation receipt, and saw finally why I never received those blue shoes."

"Look here's a copy of the confirmation receipt. While the receipt says Mrs. Ashley Loveit, the delivery address reads 1675 N.W. 8th Street. That's your address Brianna!! I typed in your address by mistake when I was filling out the on-line order form!" Ashley's tone of voice escalating with the excitement of finally solving the puzzle. Brianna now visibly more uncomfortable, was certainly not showing the same excitement of discovery Ashley was.

"You know that night when I left *Aqua* I was so upset, and Joe asked me what proof I had those shoes were mine, and I really didn't have much to go on at the time, except that you had them on your feet, but here it is!" Ashley said thrilled flapping the confirmation receipt around in the air. She felt triumphant she could set every piece of the puzzle together.

Then she continued, "So let me ask you again Brianna, one more time, did you really order those shoes on line, or did the Fedex guy just leave them on your doorstep by mistake?" Ashley ended, feeling good.

"They were so exquisite I just couldn't give them up. I don't know what came over me Ashley. I'm really sorry. I was just obsessed by those shoes. And they fitted me so perfectly. I didn't realize they were yours until the next day. I had discarded the receipt the day I tried them on. I didn't think it would hurt anyone. They were just shoes," Brianna said feeling totally trapped.

She continued on in the same quiet tone, "The next day after *Aqua*, after all the drink had worn off I thought about the shoes, and then I remembered the name on the receipt. Before I had met you I had no idea who Mrs. Ashley Loveit was. By that time, I didn't know what to do. I felt trapped. I had enjoyed your company so much, and I wanted to call to make plans with you, but I just couldn't bring myself to call Amber for your number."

"All I thought about was how much you would have hated me if I had contacted you to tell you I had taken your shoes for my own. I even gave them a name – my Heavenly Blues. " Brianna ended, speaking equally as calm, and clearly as Ashley.

Ashley burst out laughing, "Heavenly Blues!" she repeated with a frown.

She kept laughing, and laughing. She couldn't stop. Brianna began to laugh too. Soon they were both doubled over on the den floor laughing. Both women, laughing for different reasons. Brianna wasn't sure why she was laughing, except for the fact she felt relieved the truth was finally out. Conversely, Ashley did realize exactly why she was laughing, she felt sooooo much lighter, she could now see the comedy in some of life's situations, she had shed a large chunk of her past today, and was beginning to feel like a different person. She felt free.

Then Ashley pulled herself off the floor, and in a more serious tone said to Brianna, "I have to go. The sitter is leaving soon. Thank you for being honest. And don't worry Brianna I forgive you, and release you from the stress of the secret and guilt."

Brianna felt better, a bit confused by the last part of what Ashley said about the 'release' thing, but she felt it all sounded good anyway.

As Brianna walked Ashley out, the two boys ran screaming toward their mother, encircling her. "Stop! Stop! stop!" she called out to them, what is it with you both?"

"Mom, mom, mom,.." they both yelled at the same time.

"Wait," she said, "one at a time."

"Mom, he stole my blue marker. I was going to use that blue marker. It was 'my' blue marker the one Dad bought me. It's special to me, then he broke it because he got mad!" yelled the one twin.

Brianna turned to the other twin, "did you steal your brother's marker?"

"No," he responded, "I just needed it to draw in my book," the twin answered nonchalantly twisting his body this way and that.

"And did you know it was special to him?" his mother continued.

"Yes," he answered.

"What did Mommy tell you when you take other peoples things?" she said to her son.

"That sometimes those things are special to them and you don't know, and you should give it back," her son correctly responded.

At that point Brianna remembered Ashley was standing right there listening.

"Oh, my God!" said Brianna, "I can't believe I did to you what I teach my sons not to do! Oh, Ashley, I really am sorry. Please accept my apologies! Do you want to take the shoes?"

"Oh, heaven's no Brianna, I just wanted to hear the truth. Keep them, I have no place for them in my life anymore," said Ashley, and she really didn't.

Brianna walked her to the door and they parted friends, forgiveness between them. Ashley cut her imaginative cords, as she had done when she left Pam's. I release you Mrs. Ashley Loveit for hating Brianna so much for so long, for taking your blue open-toe high heel platform Gucci sandals, she said smiling to herself as she got into her car.

"Heavenly Blues?" she muttered, as she inspected her reflection in the rearview mirror before reversing out of the driveway, and burst out laughing again.

When Ashley got home, there was a message for her on facebook. Josselyn Wright had accepted her request, and left her a message on her wall. Yes, she remembered Ashley, the girl who was blinded by Joe Loveit. Ashley responded, telling Josselyn she was sorry, she had been so stupid, and asked for her forgiveness. Ashley how low have you stooped to ask for someone's forgiveness on facebook? She wondered. Ashley explained to Josselyn how she had been even more stupid several years after college and done the unthinkable; married Joe Loveit. But she had finally come to see the light, and shed him from her life. Josselyn told Ashley she was lesbian, and hence never had even the remotest interest in Joe. Strange, Ashley thought, I never even considered that at the time. She apologized once again for saying all those horrid things about

Josselyn in high school, and they parted to return to their lives, in two different parts of the globe, Ashley in Florida, U.S.A., and Josselyn in Oslo, Norway.

Pam and Brianna both felt uneasy. Although Ashley had reassured them she was fine with everything, they were still concerned she may go public with what they had done. This kind of information, if it got out, could have devastating and long term affects on their social status in Woodfield. So, when the four women met again over coffee, Amber, Brianna, Pam and Taylor, no one mentioned Ashley, and instinctively neither Amber nor Taylor pressed Pam about her meeting with Ashley the day of the birthday party. The topic of Ashley was best left to rest.

Chapter TWELVE

"I've decided on Sedona Mom," Ashley said to her mother over the phone.

"Why Sedona, Ash.? You don't even know the place. You'll have no friends. The kids will have no friends. Why Sedona?" Her mother pressed.

"Because, I like it. You and Dad took us there years ago when we were little, and out of all the memories I have, of all the places I've been to, Sedona has the sweetest memories for me. It's charming, peaceful, and there is a wonderful outdoor life for the children," Ashley replied.

"Besides," Ashley continued, "there seems to be something pulling me there. I don't know what it is. It's just something, and it doesn't seem to let go. It's like this. I was in line at the supermarket yesterday, and the store was so busy. I was about third in line at the check out, and so I picked up a magazine. I never look at this magazine, it's a nature magazine Mom! I opened it up just to look at the pictures, and there it was Sedona, this huge center page spread. It looked so beautiful, all those red rocks. And you know what else, guess the name of the journalist who wrote the article? I nearly dropped right there on the floor! Ashley Grimes. Yes, Mom she had the same name as me. Can you believe it? Yes. Mom. I've decided, Sedona."

Ashley felt good saying those words: 'I've decided, Sedona.' She felt good because she was finally making decisions. Decisions based on her feelings, and her wants, and her yearnings, and what she thought would be best for her children. And it wasn't hard, she thought to herself, because she felt it. She felt it right there, in her heart. She made a choice based on what would be good for her and her children from her heart. Yes, her head wasn't going to let it go so easily, and was repeating just what her mother was nagging on about, "but you know no-one, the kids know no-one, blah, blah, blah." But her head didn't rule her life any more, her heart did.

Astounded, Ashley would make such a huge decision based on a few magazine pictures and a journalist's name, Ashley's Mom gave it one more stab, "But Ash, Sedona is much further away from us than Florida."

Ashley wasn't buying, "Yes, I know Mom, but that is why we have airplanes. Quick, easy access to places all over the world."

Ashley's Mother surrendered, "Well, I see you've really made up your mind. When do you plan on moving, so Dad and I can come down and help you pack up?"

"No. Mom," said Ashley, "I've got this one covered. I'm a big girl, and I need to do this myself," Ashley smiled, as she remembered her own son David saying the very same thing to her months ago outside Lily's house. Perhaps she will start to do this with him too – give him space, he's growing up so fast now. Perhaps she should let him take care of a little bit more of his life, himself.

"But Ash, that's a huge job all by yourself," her mother protested.

"It will be fine," said Ashley, "If I really need help I'll call, don't worry Mom. I appreciate your offer. But this I need to do alone."

Ashley's decision felt perfect. No, matter how big the job would entail, Ashley had learned from all the hours she had spent with Lily that she could handle it. And she was going to, handle it with joy. She just knew this move would be the smoothest and happiest one she had ever made.

After saying goodbye to her mother, Ashley called the landlord, "Hi, Mr. Geld, this is Ashley. Ashley Loveit, your tenant."

She waited for his recognition, and then she proceeded, "The reason I am calling is to tell you everything has finally been settled. The divorce is final. Thank you very much for your understanding. I am planning on moving. If you can give me six more weeks I would appreciate it."

Mr. Geld was happy to oblige, and offered to help Ashley in any way she needed. Ashley felt good. Two big issues taken care of, and easily, in less than an hour – Mom and Mr. Geld. Everything reinforcing the fact, Sedona was the right choice.

Her cell phone rang in her hand. She looked down and read the name, Joe. Well, she thought, may as well make it three down in an hour.

She answered the call, "Hello, Joe."

"Hi, Ash," Joe responded. He sounded happy. She was actually pleased for him.

"You sound happy Joe," Ashley said.

"I am. I just made a huge trading coup, beat that annoying Harvard grad who sits next to me, four million dollar deal Ash, and Mel and I are going to celebrate in Bermuda for the next four days."

"Perfect Joe," Ashley said, but what she really meant was, perfect for your life Joe, but not mine. Using the high tide Joe was riding on, Ashley thought now was as good a time as ever, "Joe, we're moving. We're moving in six weeks to Sedona. I need to be sure I can make the school year for the kids. It begins the second week in August," Ashley stopped, waiting for Joe's response.

As anticipated, it didn't hit him so hard, "Oh, okay Ash. Isn't it a little soon to be moving though? I mean the divorce is just final and the kids were very confused by everything."

"No," answered Ashley, "It's the perfect time. Create some excitement for them, and we can leave some of this old, dense energy behind. Besides, I promised them a dog. They need a change, too."

"Dense energy Ash, what do you mean?" Oh, no, Ashley thought, I'm not going down that road with you.

She changed the subject, "Well," she said, "the kids have fall break in November, and a winter break in December. I can send them to you for some of those days over that time if you like. Or you can come down to stay in Sedona. There are plenty of really cute boutique hotels you can stay at. And I'm sure Mel would like it."

Joe ignored everything Ashley said, except the last sentence, "Oh, no," he said, "Mel wouldn't like Sedona. She's a hardcore city girl."

What you actually meant to say Joe, Ashley thought, was no Mel wouldn't like to be near me in Sedona. It's not Sedona she wouldn't like. I couldn't imagine anyone not liking Sedona, even city girls.

But instead Ashley said, "that's fine, you let me know," she then added, "And have a good stay in Bermuda," hoping to end the call. And of course it did.

"Thanks Ash. Can you have the kids call me tonight. I want to say goodbye to them before I leave for Bermuda tomorrow."

"Of, course," Ashley responded.

∞∞

The next few weeks Ashley was very busy. She had to contact and organize packers, movers, realtors, and deal with schools. There was no end to her list. She called various charitable organizations and had them pick up furniture and clothes from the house, furniture pieces she and Joe had chosen together, or furniture that just reminded her of Joe. All the while she burnt incense and played Buddha chants in an attempt to keep the energy in the house clean with all the comings and goings of so many people. Everything Ashley did, she did with love in her heart. Just as Lily had explained to her. If you can't do it with love in your heart, then don't do it, or change your attitude towards it. See it in a good way. Look for the positive in doing it. What are the energies trying to tell you? Why do you need to do something?

Ashley was beginning to love life in a big way. She happily dropped David off at school in the mornings, Joe, Jr. at pre-school, and she always welcomed into her home the daytime nanny who took care of Amber. Nina had left for a job which brought her more money. Pampering the daytime nanny with all kinds of small surprises, like Ohm necklaces, or wind chimes made Ashley feel good. The nanny, Bagar, was from Nepal, and Ashley loved to get into long conversations with her about her homeland, and how the Buddha's in the mountains of Nepal lived their lives. Ashley was now aware of every person in her life, and always tried to determine why her life had interacted with theirs. Even if her path crossed someone's at the organic farmer's market, and they only exchanged a few words. Why did I meet them? What message were they meant to give me? What message did I give them? When her mind wasn't occupied with these spiritual thoughts they were occupied with practical ones of her impending move.

Two weeks before she was scheduled to move she called Pam, "Pam," she said, "Hi. How are you?"

Pam sounded shocked, as expected, "Ash, I haven't heard from you in ages. I thought you hated me...." Although, Ashley could feel Pam's wound was still raw from their conversation a few weeks back, there was still the old familiar *I* focus. It was always about Pam. What Pam did or didn't do, what Pam was given or not given. A little time away from it all, and being with Lily, Ashley could see it clearly now, from a full birds eye view. How far away she stood today, from all of this past.

Ashley stopped her in her tracks, "No, Pam, I'm calling to tell you I'm moving in two weeks. I'm going to live in Sedona."

"Yeah, I heard you were moving, the kids told me. I just didn't know where. Why Sedona?" asked Pam.

"Long story," answered Ashley and she continued, "but the other reason why I called was because I was packing and found this cute little outfit you left at my house which belongs to your daughter, and I wanted to return it to you. Will you be home in an hour?" Pam perked up, she was thrilled Ashley wanted to come over, she still wanted to be her friend even after everything she had done to her.

"Actually, I will because I have some packages to drop home for the housekeeper, Mira," answered Pam.

"Great," said Ashley, "I will see you then."

"Ash," Pam said a little more softly, "would you like to stay for some coffee like we always used to do?"

Coffee, maybe thought Ashley, but like we used to do, all that gossip, no, not any more. "I think coffee would be nice Pam, thank you. But I can't stay too long, I have a laundry list of things to attend to."

"Well, can't the housekeeper do those things for you while you have coffee with me?" Pam killed the moment.

"I'll see you soon Pam, bye," Ashley shook her head as she pressed the red 'end call" button on her Blackberry.

An hour later, Ashley rang Pam's doorbell.

"Ash!" Pam shrieked as she opened the door, throwing her arms around Ashley tightly, and sending the traditional two kisses into the air, one on either side of Ashley's head. Kissing one another anywhere on the face was a huge taboo with the Woodfield women, because it was a make up destroyer. Kisses destroyed beauty. Showing someone love and affection destroyed beauty. How incredibly backwards that sounds to me now Ashley thought.

"Hi, Pam," was all Ashley could say after being released from Pam's grip.

"Ash, you don't look so good," said Pam, "You have no makeup on, your hair's a mess, and isn't that the sweat suit we bought together two years ago?"

"Wow," said Ashley, "that's a nice welcome."

"Oh, I'm sorry Ash. But are you okay?" asked Pam, their conversation months ago washed away from her mind.

"Pam," Ashley said, "I have never felt better in my whole life," and she truly meant it.

"Here's the outfit," Ashley said handing a small bag to Pam.

Pam took it without saying anything, and then she said "Come in Ash., come let's go up to my room and have some coffee," she shuffled Ashley into the house, up the stairs, and into her bedroom. On the way, she leaned her head back and yelled, "Mira, two coffees in my room please."

"I have so much to tell you Ash. You just wouldn't believe it. That chick with the double DD's from 1112. She's a scream. We have had so many fun shopping dates together. Oh, and there is this new store that opened up on Atlantic avenue, to die for…" Pam rattled on.

Ashley went numb. Pam was so busy 'filling Ashley in' she hadn't even noticed Ashley wasn't looking at her or listening anymore. She was looking around Pam's bedroom instead. She noticed there seemed to be one of everything in her room. One vase, a picture on the wall had one solitary figure in it, there was one chair, one dresser, even one family photo with everyone in it, minus John of course.

"Pam," Ashley said, "do you miss your old life with John? Do you want to find someone new?"

Pam stopped in midsentence, "Ash., what are you talking about, are you even listening to me?" She suddenly realized Ashley's entire body was turned away from her.

"Do you want to find someone new?" Ashley repeated.

"Oh, my God Ash, how can you even ask me that, you know that Mr. Right has always been my dream."

"Well, look around your bedroom Pam. There is one of everything, except for the pillows on your bed. How can you meet someone new if you are only focused on one. If you want love to enter your life you have to reflect it, all around you. You need to replace this art piece on the wall and get one with two people in it, preferably a man and a woman. You should look for a set of two vases, change out the large dresser and get two smaller ones."

"But my decorator chose that dresser, Ash."

"Exactly," said Ashley, "and, is your decorator in a wonderfully happy relationship? No. He's still looking for that perfect partner!"

"And you need plants in this room Pam, to promote good health. Hold on," Ashley left the room. She ran down the stairs, passing Mira on the way up with the two coffees.

"Oh, hi you must be Mira," Ashley said stopping for an instant.

"Yes," said Mira, in the usual bored tone, like all of Pam's employees.

"I'm Ashley, and it is nice to meet you," Ashley said friendly, ignoring her mood, and then proceeded down the stairs. Ashley picked up the two huge orchid plants she saw in the foyer when she arrived, one in each arm, and then ran back up the stairs.

"Here," she said returning to the room, her arms full holding the two plants, and passing Mira as she was leaving the room.

"Thanks," Ashley said to Mira.

Surprisingly, Mira said, "you're welcome," in a very pleasant tone. Pam raised her eyebrows, amazed. She had never heard Mira be so nice.

"Two. You need to place them here, right here," Ashley laid the plants gently down on a ledge at the foot of the bed. Pam just stood there. She had nothing to say. A first. Well, a first other than their conversation a few weeks back. A first during a Pam's gossip session, I guess, thought Ashley.

"Look," Ashley said referring to the two orchids at the foot of the bed.

"I don't know what to say," articulated Pam. Then she said, "But the flowers are yellow and purple they don't match my room."

"They're flowers Pam, beautiful flowers, they don't need to match! They represent good health, and they're together. See, there are two of them?" Ashley said, "You, know perhaps this is what you need, someone who is totally mismatched to you who will show you a different kind of life, a life full of outdoor activities, and…" Ashley looked over at Pam. She could see she wasn't making much headway. She then said.,"I'm sorry Pam this has been fun, but I have to go. I still have so much to do today."

"But Ash, I haven't even told you about this cute guy that I met at…"

"I can't stay," Ashley interrupted, "But I'm glad I got to see you before leaving anyway," said Ashley.

Pam was silent as she followed Ashley to the front door. As they reached the door Pam spoke sadly facing the back of Ashley, "I'm going to miss you Ash, we've known each other since high school. I moved here because you were my best friend in the whole world, and you said how great Florida was."

Ashley turned to face Pam, "There is a part of me that will miss you too, Pam. But try and be happy for me. And I'm glad you have made a new friend, with what's her name, the one with the double DD's? She will make it easier for you."

"Yes, but she is not my Ash, and I *am* happy for you, Ash," said Pam.

"I'm nobody's Ash, Pam. I belong to myself, and you belong to yourself," Ashley said firmly.

Then as Ashley turned, and stepped off the front door threshold Pam said, "I wish I was like you Ash. As brave as you, that I could move away and find another place too, and be happy like you."

Ashley stopped, and turned around to fully face Pam, "*You* are as brave as me Pam, and *you* will move Pam, when *you* decide the time is right for *you*. And it is not in the move Pam. It doesn't matter where you live in the world, it's about *you*. Learning to belong to *you*." Ashley gave Pam a soft kiss on the cheek, swung around and continued down the path to her car. This chapter in her life was done.

∞∞

A few days before they were scheduled to leave for Sedona, Ashley had her car shipped ahead by train. She needed to have a car there when she arrived. Her realtor in Sedona was kind enough to receive her car on the other side, and scheduled to pick her up from the airport.

Once her car had been shipped she had to rely on taxis or her nanny Bagar for rides. Luckily, the children had finished school for the year. So, the taking and fetching to and from schools was no longer an issue. The boxes and furniture were picked up by the movers, and Ashley took Joe, Jr. and Madison around the neighborhood to say their formal goodbye's to their respective friends. She had stopped going to the Woodfield Club House ages ago. And a small goodbye party at home was out of the question.

But there were two people Ashley and David each had to say goodbye to before leaving. As it was for David, it was for Ashley, and they dreaded it, Lily and Ari. Lily was one person Ashley always wanted in her life. Lily had changed her life, and she was always there for her. She reminisced the many hours they chatted quietly across the candle lit table under the moonlight, discussing abstract concepts until three am. Lily had been the Divine Intervention Ashley needed at such a desperate time in her life. She had turned a corner in her life with Lily by her side. One which was so deeply personal it would be very hard to even explain to another human being. One only Lily truly understood.

Lily and Ari stopped by the house the night before they were due to leave. They wanted to say goodbye, "I'm going to miss you so much Lily. How will I ever find a friend like you again?" Ashley said, tears streaming down her cheeks.

"Oh, Ashley," Lily said, "it's not about replacing me, it's about adding new people, new Souls to your life who will enrich your life, and help you grow and understand yourself that little bit more."

"I'm so afraid though. Do you think I will meet someone again like Joe? I mean be attracted to another Joe?" asked Ashley.

"Well, that depends on you Ashley. Have you grown beyond the Joe's of this world, or do you still need them to grow? Remember, sometimes we meet people years later after they have grown and we have grown, and we are able to be together in a much more harmonious manner than we ever had before, or we meet people similar to others we have known, but more evolved than those we had once known. But never be afraid Ashley. You are always protected. Besides, you are ready. You are ready, the energies tell me, to pass the healing on. You have gone through a great deal but you made it to the other side. Now it's your turn to help someone else who will be in the same situation you once found yourself in. This is a blessing Ashley. Having the opportunity to help just one person in your entire life, is a blessing. So, be blessed Ashley," Lily said. Ashley noticed that in her entire monologue Lily had not used one 'I' word like Pam had done a couple of weeks back. Or let me check myself here, Ashley thought, like I used to do myself when I was part of Pam's world. That existence seemed as if it was a decade ago.

"Will we see one another again?" Ashley asked sadly as they stood on the curb next to Lily's car.

"Sure, we would love to come out your way sometime. Our paths crossed once, doesn't mean they may never cross again. Even though it may not feel like it to you, you enriched my life as well Ashley, and for this I am deeply grateful, and I thank you. Every Soul you help, helps you in return. Sometimes, in the most weird, and unexpected ways. It's kind of like a hidden reward system actually. I love you Ashley. Just be happy. And always paint. Life can be a rollercoaster ride Ashley, just ride it, don't fight it." Lily hugged Ashley tightly, sweetly kissed her on both cheeks while holding her head in her hands. She then got into her car, started the engine, waived good-bye and was gone.

Ashley wasn't sure if she would see Lily ever again. But, maybe David and Ari's friendship would always keep her wish to reunite alive.

After they left, Ashley stood for a long time at the curb, just staring into space, numb, tears streaming down her face. David joined her, and she slid her arm across his shoulder, and pulled him closer towards her. Both were feeling the same pain. Neither of them said anything. They didn't have to.

∞∞

  The day Ashley sat seated in the rear of the limousine heading for the airport, and drove out of the Woodfield gated community for the last time, she felt a surge of freedom, a gratitude for how far she had come, and an excitement for the new which awaited her. This was a very different Ashley to the one who had moved into Woodfield a few years ago.

  As previously planned, she sent the children to stay with their grandparents for a week or two, until she could secure a temporary place for all of them to live, and to look for a house they could call home. Sedona was just as she remembered. Tucked away amongst the most exquisite red rock topography. It sat at the mouth of the Oak Creek Canyon and could only be reached by a sheer, winding, single lane road carved into the red rock cliffs. Traveling along this road gives one the impression of winding down into a very deep isolated valley town, but in actual fact Sedona is 4,400 feet above sea level, a town with a population of about 11,000. Adding to the natural beauty of the red rocks are Sycamores, Cypress, Juniper and Ponderosa Pine trees.

  Although, originally a small agricultural community, Sedona's natural landscape soon lured an assortment of artists, and quickly became an artist's sanctuary which culminated in what became known as the Cowboy Artists of America. Joining the artists came the New Age believers, who turned Sedona into a hot bed of alternative therapies. Mountain bikers also discovered Sedona, and now congregate certain times of the year to ride the red rocks. Signs, indicating numerous hiking trailheads, is but another area attraction. Sedona sits at the base of an irregular row of cliffs, has four delightfully mild seasons, plenty of sunshine, peace, quiet, and clean, fresh, dry meditative air. It is for all of these reasons, and more, Ashley felt so attracted to Sedona.

She settled into her hotel room at the L'Auberge de Sedona, in time to sit back, relax, and enjoy a sunset drink with Maya, her realtor. The two of them sat together on the hotel balcony looking out at the red stone formations which totally surrounded them. The red rocks were glowing in brilliant orange and red, illuminated by the setting sun. It was a moment of peace Ashley loved. Both women were dressed in relaxed loose cotton clothing, Ashley in white, Maya in red.

"How long have you lived here in Sedona, Maya?" She asked.

"Oh, all my life Ashley. My ancestors were one of the pioneering families who settled here in 1877, around when the post office was established," Maya responded.

"That is a long time Maya," Ashley commented.

"Are you an artist Maya?"

"No, my husband is though. I prefer more of the healing alternative arts. I'm a Reiki master, and I also dabble in other energy healing techniques. Which reminds me, you have a very nice, well balanced aura around you, Ashley," said Maya.

"Maya you have no idea how long and what I have had to go through to reach that nice well balanced aura," responded Ashley laughing lightly.

"I bet," said Maya, and this time they both laughed.

The next morning Maya joined Ashley for breakfast at Oak Creek, a stream which ran along the edge of the hotel's property. The hotel restaurant had set up a dozen tables of all sizes right at the edge of the creek. The two ate breakfast, and drank coffee as the stream rippled by. The water was cool and clear and you could see all the smooth rounded rocks scattered beneath its surface. It was a little piece of Heaven on Earth, thought Ashley.

"I have lots to show you today, Ashley," said Maya.

"Oh, Maya you have no idea how excited I am."

By the end of the day Ashley had found the perfect home for her and the children. It was simple, practical, and perfectly located, with views of the gorgeous red rocks from every window in the house. The house was raised high enough so Ashley could stand her easel out in the front garden and be able to paint a panoramic view of the rosy sandstone cliffs. Off in the distance, one could see the forests of Juniper and Ponderosa pine trees. Her neighbors were far enough away to keep her home private, and yet close enough to ward off any feelings of isolation. She wanted her children to be able to play with the other neighborhood children.

The home was vacant, and because it was a cash deal, Ashley, having enough money from the divorce settlement, could expedite the closing, and the house became hers within a matter of days. Through Maya, Ashley organized to have the house spiritually cleansed by a renown local psychic. She then proceeded to call everyone to begin the settling in process. The kids were as excited to see their new home in Sedona, as she was to show it to them. They settled in quickly, and life was full.

Two weeks after they moved in, Ashley was lounging on her couch in the living room experiencing life in the moment. All the doors were open to the outside where the two younger children were running around and playing in the garden sprinklers. David was lying in his room lazily video chatting with Ari on his laptop. The doorbell rang. Ashley sat up. She wasn't expecting anyone. Maya said she might stop by, but not until much later in the day. Maybe Maya's plans changed, she thought.

Ashley got up, and casually made her way to the front door. She opened the door. Before her stood a very tall, dark, handsome stranger holding what looked like a homemade apple pie in one hand, and the hand of a little girl in the other.

"Hello," said the stranger with the sea foam green eyes.

"Hello," Ashley responded, a little curious as to who this person was at her door.

"We're from next door, and wanted to welcome you to the neighborhood. Here, it's an apple pie. We picked the apples ourselves," said the handsome stranger, offering the pie to Ashley.

Ashley took it. "Thank you very much," she said, "My name is Ashley."

"Nice to meet you Ashley, my name is Jake, Jake Love, but you can call me Jay…"

At that moment Ashley almost fainted, and nearly dropped the apple pie.

"Oh, I'm sorry, are you alright?" Jay asked looking very concerned, and a little confused.

"No, no, no I'm sorry," said Ashley, "I don't know what came over me. I'm fine thank you." She was holding the pie with both hands now.

Ashley looked down at the little girl, she hadn't stopped smiling since they had arrived.

"We live next door," said the little girl, "alone." Emphasizing the word *alone*. "My name is Brianna," she said, "Brianna Love."

"Nice to meet you Ms. Brianna Love," Ashley said smiling.

But it wasn't Brianna's smile which was capturing Ashley's attention. It was what was on her feet. She wore a pair of blue platform sandals, almost identical to the blue high heel open-toe Gucci platform sandals she had once ordered off line.

"I knew a Brianna as pretty as you once, and she had the same pretty blue shoes you have Brianna," said Ashley, totally stunned at what she was witnessing right before her eyes.

"Can I see what the other kids are doing outside?" Brianna asked coyly.

"Oh, yes, of course I'm sorry how rude of me, please do come in and join us."

Ashley closed the front door smiling, remembering Lily's words: *And then sometimes we meet people similar to others we have known, but more evolved than those we had once known.* Ashley had reached the end of the chapter with Joe, perhaps she was about to turn over a new leaf with Jay.

Only time would tell, and she had plenty of it. Her whole life in fact.

"Any one for fresh apple pie and icecream?" she called out to the children.

THE END

Always Remember

It is not the happenings per se which shape our lives. Rather, it is how we think about those happenings that shape us.

Hope you had as much fun reading this book,

as I had creating it.

To communicate with the author: bevgoodman@bellsouth.net

Proof

12602104R00143

Made in the USA
Charleston, SC
15 May 2012